Natalie Roers

Based on the Screenplay by Natalie Roers and Mali Elfman

Agnos Publishing

Honolulu, HI, USA

2017

Published in the USA by Aignos Publishing LLC
an imprint of Savant Books and Publications
2630 Kapiolani Blvd #1601
Honolulu, HI 96826
http://www.savantbooksandpublications.com

Printed in the USA

Edited by Eleonor Gardner
Cover Art by Kellie Dennis | Book Cover by Design
Author Photo by Cory Eglseder

13-digit ISBN: 978-0-9970020-6-5

First Edition: June 2017
Library of Congress Control Number: 2017940714

To Mali.

Special thanks to
Sari Prince and my wonderful support system of family and
friends. I am such a fortunate woman.

Dear Reader,

This novel would not be complete were it not for the significant storyline contributions of one, Mali Elfman. You see, when I first started writing this book, I ended up shelving it about halfway through, for no particular good reason. Sometime later, quite out of the blue, I received a phone call to come work on a film set where I first met Mali. Did I mention the film set was in Alabama--where this story was set--even before me and Mali's serendipitous meeting there? It's a place I'd never even personally been before. We became friends and it was with Mali's help and encouragement that I picked this story back up and finished it with her as a screenplay. So the first half of the book inspired the screenplay, but the second half of the screenplay inspired the rest of the book. It's a weird story of fate that could only be attached to a story like this. And I love it. And I love her for it. Thank you, Mali.

Chapter 1

Derek Fisher heard his mother's voice inside his head as he came to a standstill in front of the big, brick home on Grandview Drive. *Always look around you. You remember that, boy. 'Cause even if you ain't lookin' at them, if someone's gonna get ya, you can bet they've been lookin' at you.*

Derek took in his surroundings. The streets were empty and it would be getting light soon. But for the moment, the beautiful suburban, Southern neighborhood was still fast asleep. He'd walked through heavy rain all night trying to find this place—the place he'd first seen with his mother nearly six months prior—the home with the dark red shutters, muted brick, and a painted sign by the front door that read "The Scotts."

A small lamp glowed warmly from inside one of the Scotts' main windows. Derek felt himself moving down the driveway toward it, as if the light would be able to melt the chill right out of his body; if he could just get close enough to it. It was an unusually cold October night by Northern Alabama standards, and Derek's wet, ripped up T-shirt and jeans clung to his thin teenage frame as he moved. He stopped though, when he reached a fancy black car parked in front of the home's spacious attached garage.

Derek shivered in the driveway as he gazed out over the Scotts' small, square lawn at a figure coming into focus through the illuminated living room window of the home. The figure in the window paced back and forth slowly, in a methodical fashion. *One of the Scotts*, Derek mused. Whoever it was, they appeared to be holding some sort of large package at their side. Derek swallowed nervously and looked up the driveway toward the street again. The neighborhood was still. He also noticed there was a thin swath of woods that circled the Scotts' home, protecting him from any prying eyes. The neighbors surely wouldn't be able to see him this far down the driveway.

But as Derek turned around to look back at the house, his heart stopped. The figure in the window was now looking right back at him! At the shocking realization, Derek's body snapped down to the ground instinctively. His eyes wide and panicked, remained fixed on the window. The figure he had been watching was a woman, and the package he thought she was carrying by her side wasn't a package at all—it was a baby strapped into some sort of carrier.

With the carrier on her hip, the woman pressed her forehead against the windowpane. She cupped her free hand over her eyes, obviously straining to see out into the darkness. She paused eyeing the bottom of the driveway where Derek was hiding. He remained crouched on the ground next to the fancy black car, frozen, as the woman began to scream.

"Oh my god, Jason! The car! The car!" the woman yelled.

Derek jerked his head to the left and looked once more at the shiny, black car parked next to him in the driveway. Did she think he was breaking into the car? Derek's blood started to pump faster as the garage door in front of him roared to life. It made a horrible grinding squeal as it opened. Popping up, Derek quickly ducked around the side of the garage where he flattened himself against the wall.

"Shit!" He heard a deep man's voice exclaim from inside the open garage. "Come on, really?!"

Derek pressed his palms flat against the rough, wet brick of the home, praying he wouldn't be found. But the man who yelled did not run after him. Instead, Derek listened as he started the car in the driveway and pulled it forward into the garage.

"Oh my god, I'm so sorry. I can't believe I forgot to roll the windows up!"

The voice of the woman Derek had seen inside now joined the man's behind the wall. "Is it wet?"

The engine shut off and the man called back to her. "Grab me a towel, will ya?" He cursed and grumbled a few more re-marks that Derek couldn't quite make out over the rain.

Derek's fifteen-year-old body trembled as he let out a sigh

of relief. The couple wasn't upset about him. They were upset about the windows of their car being left open in the rain overnight! He hadn't been seen. He was safe.

From inside the garage, the man yelled, "Hurry up with that towel, will ya?"

When there was no answer, the man's voice grew louder and more urgent. "Lauren! Where are you?! My butt's soakin' wet here!"

Once again, there was no reply.

"Lauren! I'm a freakin' mess!" the man screamed. "Seriously, how long's it take to get a damn tow…"

Just then, the woman's voice cut him off before he could finish. "You think *you're* a mess?! Look at me!"

On the other side of the wall, Derek braced himself at the sound of their raised voices. He knew very well what came with raised voices, but it didn't come. Instead, the strangest thing happened.

The man—Jason, as she had called him—let out a sort of chuckle. "What happened to you?"

"Landon just spit up all over the kitchen."

Jason's laughter grew louder.

"It's not funny," Lauren said.

"It's kind of funny."

"It's everywhere. Look at this! It's even in my hair!"

The man laughed harder.

"It's not funny!" Lauren tried to argue, but her voice

cracked and a giggle escaped from her lips.

There was a slight hesitation and then Lauren's laughter rose all the way up to meet Jason's. Inside, the baby began to cry, interrupting their moment.

"It's nice to hear you laugh again," Jason said, then paused thoughtfully. Derek listened on as Jason closed the car door with a thud. "Don't worry about the car. We can put some towels in there later. Why don't you go hop in the shower and I'll perform an exorcism on Landon while you're in there."

"Really, you like this?" Lauren teased. "Well, come here and give Momma a big hug then."

Derek leaned forward off the wall. The interaction between Jason and Lauren bewildered him, as a playful dance he couldn't see broke out in the garage from somewhere behind him. *What are these crazy people doing?* He'd never in his life heard adults behave this way.

"Get away from me woman! I don't want that stuff on me!"

"No, really. I wanna give you a big ole' bear hug and show you just how much I love you!" she joked.

"Isn't it enough you left the windows down on my brand-new car?"

The couple's laughter trailed back inside the house. Derek shook his head. It didn't make sense. Had he missed something? Their car was messed up. Why were they both laughing?

Moving down the side of the house, Derek tried to see if

he could get a glimpse of the couple who were now inside. A series of windows ran down the side of the home, but they were all set too high off the ground for him to see into. Derek jumped to see if that would help, but all he managed to do was set off a motion security light attached to the back corner of the house. Derek startled at the light. He quickly ducked around the back of the home, afraid of being seen. In the backyard, Derek discovered a steep set of stairs that led up to a high and large wooden deck attached to the back of the house. Going up the steps seemed too risky to him. It was too close. The couple would surely see him if he did that. That's when Derek noticed the door. It was at the base of the stairs leading up to the deck. The door was made of wood, its white paint just beginning to peel. He immediately knew what it was—a crawl space door. The water table in Alabama was fairly high, plus the soil tended to be hard-packed clay, so most homes weren't built with basements beneath them. Instead, they were lifted high off the ground with large unfinished "rooms" underneath called "crawl spaces." Crawl spaces were usually big, but not good for much more than storing lawn equipment.

The wind kicked up and Derek's mouth fell open as he watched the crawl space door swing open in front of him. The motion light he had set off before shone brightly down on the opening like a light from Heaven. He had never slept in a home that wasn't abandoned before. It wasn't something he'd have ever thought to do on his own, but damn it if it didn't seem like the house was inviting him in. Placing his hand on the open door, Derek noticed the empty latch where a padlock should have been hanging. He wouldn't stay long, he reasoned. Besides it wasn't like the couple above would need to come down for anything in this kind of weather, would they? Shaking his dirty, tangled hair away from his eyes, Derek stepped inside and wedged the door of the crawl space closed behind him.

It was pitch dark in the crawl space and the air around him felt thick and moist. As Derek took a seat on the ground, a heavy plastic tarp shifted beneath him. It felt good to sit. Stifling a cough with his fist, Derek looked up into the dark. The couple's footsteps moved restlessly about overhead. He could hear them talking as well, but their voices were too muffled to make out anything they were saying. He leaned his head back and exhaled a deep breath that rattled with infection, a small movement that brought with it a wave of crushing tiredness. As Derek's eyes adjusted to the dark, his eyelids became heavier and time between blinks slowed. In fact, by the time he noticed the movement at the far end of the crawl space, he questioned whether or not his eyes were even open.

As if he couldn't help himself, he softly called out, "Mom?"

The shadow moved again, but this time it was accompanied by a loud and terrible cackle. As Derek listened to the laughter reverberate throughout the small, dark confines of the crawl space, he felt his small hopes sink before they even had a chance to set sail.

She had found him.

Derek shut his eyes tightly, hoping the return of darkness might be enough to block out the memories, but it was no use. His memories were just as strong as the smell of bleach that now cut through the musty air in the crawl space. When he opened his eyes, he was six years old again.

"Take off your clothes," she ordered.

Derek lay shivering next to the toilet. He was old enough by now to know how important it was not to disobey his mother, but his body was so weak from throwing up that he kept falling over every time he tried to move.

"Goddamn it, get up." Her many cheap plastic bangles jangled on her arms as she entered the bathroom. "You're acting like a little baby."

Derek put his arm up on top of the toilet seat and tried to hoist himself up. He had almost made it to his feet before the tiny little stars overtook his vision. On the way down, his head cracked against the side of the porcelain sink and he heard his mother shriek as he landed and grabbed onto the bottom of her legs.

"Idiot!" She screamed kicking him off of her. "Now there's blood on the floor! Do you know what kinds of diseases you can get from that?"

Derek's hand shook as he lifted it to his forehead. "Sorry,

ma'am," he mumbled.

"You're sorry?!" Her voice was shrill and barely con-trolled. "What good's that do me, huh? I'm probably going to die from all the germs you brought in here. Is that what you want?" she screamed. "You want me to die?!"

"No, ma'am."

"You goddamn right you don't. Who would wanna take care of you like this?"

His mother turned her thin frame to the side to check her jeans and white half top for any "contamination." When she was sure she was clean, she grabbed a hairband off the sink and in one elegant movement, tied her long, brown hair back into a ponytail. "Only a mother would put up with crap like this."

Derek could only muster another quiet, "Yes, ma'am" as she ripped off his two-sizes-too-small, superhero underwear, grabbed him under the armpits, and lifted him into the tub. The splash of the scalding hot water jolted him back to life. He let out a yelp as he tried to fight against her, but his mother only pushed him back down by his shoulders.

"Oh, come on," she moaned. "It's not *that* bad."

The overwhelming scent of bleach made his eyes water and Derek could only whimper as his mother poured what hadn't already been dumped in the bathwater over his head. She then picked up the scrub brush she used for cleaning the floors and went to work on his skin.

"Lift your arms," she instructed.

The brush was shaped like an iron and had hard white plastic bristles. They felt like a million tiny razor blades cutting and tearing across his flesh as she scrubbed furiously back and forth. Each swipe of the brush created a large angry section of raised skin. His mother was nothing if not thorough though. The patches of red skin gradually connected together until his entire body took on the same uniformed puffy, red quality. "There. That's better now, isn't it?"

Derek only nodded, praying his compliance would make it end.

"This'll kill whatever the bleach doesn't," she assured him. "Those germs can't hide from us, can they?"

"No, ma'am."

"Can they?" she asked again, this time with more enthusiasm.

"No, ma'am," he said louder.

Her dark, brown, overly lined eyes were empty, like she was caught up in some distant memory, but his agreement appeared to have a calming effect. Over the next few minutes, the pressure of the brush lightened and the time between strokes slowed. When she was done, Derek's mother leaned back on her heels and stared at her son in the tub. Her voice quieted and took on a serious "knowing" tone. "Disease has wiped out entire civilizations, you know."

Derek didn't know what to say. He just sat there and shivered with his arms wrapped around his knees. He tried to hold her gaze, but his eyes fell back to the bath water. Derek could feel himself sinking under the intensity of Angela's eyes on him as she studied his face. Searching for a life raft, Derek focused in on a bead of water that was forming on the tub's leaky faucet. When the weight of the water became too heavy, it fell with a plunk into the water around his toes. Derek was envious of the water's ability to fall away like that; when the pressure became too much. But like a cruel joke in sync with his private inner thoughts, another bead of water immediately began to form in its place. He was waiting for it to drop when his mother suddenly lurched forward toward him, stopping only about an inch from his face. Derek felt himself flinch as she spoke.

"You did a good job," she said. "They almost got us, but we were just too darn smart for 'em, weren't we?" She brushed a wet lock of his hair to the side and smiled. His hair was deep brown, just like hers. Derek tried to smile back. She rarely touched him like that. He knew he wasn't a baby anymore, and he would never tell her this, but he thought it felt really good.

"There's just one more thing." Derek's mother grabbed the jug of bleach off of the floor. Dipping the bottle into the tub, she gathered some water into the mouth of the container, and then replaced the cap. Angela gave the bottle a good shake. "There's still some left!" she chirped. Derek watched with curiosity as his mother opened the bottle and poured a small amount of the bleach-water mixture into the cap.

She held it out for him to take. "Bottom's up!"

Derek's eyes widened. He knew kids weren't supposed to drink cleaning supplies. In his kindergarten class, they had spent a whole week drawing "Mr. Yuck" posters. The kids were even given stickers to take home of the little green face that warned of poison.

"What?" his mother asked innocently.

The idea of drinking bleach was far more frightening to Derek than any bath she could ever give him.

"You have more germs on the inside than you do on the outside, right?" she asked.

He thought about it a moment. Derek knew he couldn't argue with his mother, and what she was saying *did* make pretty good sense, but he was still scared. His mother nodded in approval as Derek reached out a shaky hand for the cap and brought it to his lips.

Sticking out her tongue in a playful fashion, his mom splashed a little water at him. Derek smiled—a real, full smile. His mom's name was Angela. She always told Derek she was named that because she was born with the face of an angel. Through the steamy, bleach filled haze of the bathroom, Derek couldn't help but agree. She did. She looked exactly like an angel.

Chapter 2

Beep! Beep! Beep!

Derek's eyes flew open at the sound of the alarm. There was a rush of footsteps overhead followed by the muffled sounds of voices yelling back and forth to one another. It took Derek a moment to recall where he was.

Birds were chirping outside. Brilliant sunshine poured in through the air vents of the crawl space, creating beautiful checkered patterns of light on the ground around him. The volume of the alarm grew to a piercing scream as a window was opened somewhere above him. Derek heard the woman—he remembered her name was Lauren—yell at the man, Jason, to open the door. Inside the crawl space, Derek leapt to his feet, ready to run. The back door to the house above swung open and the heavy fall of a man's feet could be heard thundering down the stairs toward the backyard.

"Go on, get!" The man yelled to some unseen creature. "Get out!"

There was a loud thump inside and the alarm stopped.

"Got it!" Lauren yelled triumphantly. "Jason?! What are you doing down there? Come back in here and get the bacon. I need you to dump it outside. It smells like something was dang burned alive in here."

Derek could now smell the faint smell of smoke wafting into the crawl space.

"Get!" he heard Jason call again.

A telephone began to ring inside, adding to the morning chaos.

"Speaking of burning something alive," Jason said as he jogged back up the steps to his wife. "That damn cat from next door is confusing Landon's sandbox for a litter box again."

Jason grabbed the pan of burned bacon from his wife in the kitchen. "You gonna get the phone?"

"Nah, let the machine get it. It's my mom."

Inside the crawl space, Derek listened to Jason's footsteps as he brought the bacon out of the kitchen and down the deck stairs to throw out. Inside the house, Lauren opened more windows. Unable to see the couple directly as they moved around him, playing out their lives, Derek noticed subtle nuances in their voices. Both Lauren and Jason spoke with the vocabulary of southerners but their nondescript accents made Derek assume that either they or their parents had been transplants to the area. He wondered about all the places they had seen before moving to Grandview Drive and even wondered if he'd ever see those places himself. Lauren's voice matched what he had seen of her—her medium tone was smart and playfully sarcastic; Jason's deep baritone voice was strong but full of warmth.

"This isn't what I meant when I said I wanted my bacon crispy," Jason joked as he opened the lid to a large plastic trash can that was stored under the deck at the foot of the deck stairs.

"I said I was sorry!" Lauren called through one of the open windows. There was now an edge to her voice that hadn't been there before. Only Derek heard the heavy exhale from Jason in response to his wife.

From deep within the house their baby began to cry.

"Jason? Can you come get Landon?" Lauren yelled.

There was heaviness in Jason's pause before he called back, "Could you maybe bring him to the door for me?"

There was absolutely no hesitation in Lauren's response to her husband. "Don't do this to me right now, Jason! I am not in the mood for this!"

From inside the crawl space, Derek tried to envision this man, Jason, as he walked begrudgingly back up the stairs to his wife. He closed his eyes and imagined Lauren at the top of the stairs, taking the now empty pan from him and frowning as Jason moved past her and into the house. Derek closed his eyes to help him better tune into their movements. In his mind's eye, Derek could perfectly picture Jason carrying their son out to where Lauren stood by the open doorway, so that they could all breathe in the fresh, smoke-free air together.

"Shhh. There now," Jason comforted the baby. "Weather's nice this morning," Jason said, trying to change the tone between him and his wife. "That warm front came in just like they said it would. We can keep those windows open all week."

"Da!" the baby cooed.

"Wook at that widdle face." The man's voice took on a strange high-pitched quality that Derek had never heard before.

"Why don't you take him for a walk 'til it airs out inside?" Lauren said. "I'm gonna head to the store, get some muffins or something."

"You don't have to go to the store."

"I know. I want to."

"Lauren, I was just kidding about the bacon."

"I know."

"You okay?"

"Jesus, Jason. I'm fine! I just want some damn muffins! Is that okay?"

"Whoa," Jason drew Landon's head to his chest, covering his ears. "Not in front of the baby."

"I'm fine," Lauren whispered loudly.

"I didn't say you weren't."

"I know. It's just…" Lauren paused as she looked at her baby. "It's just…"

"What?"

"I'm sorry," Lauren breathed out hard. "I'm sorry. I didn't mean to snap at you. Between wrecking the car and then my mom calling again..."

"She just loves you."

"I know, but I'm not five," Lauren countered. "I don't need her calling me twenty times a day. Anyway, between that and almost burning down the house..."

"So breakfast burned. We're fine."

"I know that. Don't." Lauren held a hand up in front of her. "Don't try to placate me. Okay? You have no idea what it's like to feel like everyone is constantly judging you. Like every little thing you do is being analyzed."

Lauren might have been apologizing, but everything about her screamed she was spoiling for a fight.

Jason paused, carefully. "So what you're saying is..." Derek found that not only had he opened his eyes during the argument, but he was now leaning forward on his toes in anticipation of how Jason would finish. "...you want to go to the store and buy some muffins?"

The joke completely leveled the building tension.

Lauren smirked. "Yes, that is exactly what I'm saying."

Inside the crawl space, Derek smiled.

"I'm sorry, baby," Lauren said, leaning forward and kissing Landon on the cheek. "Mommy's a little on edge these days. You can tell your therapist all about it when you're older, just like the rest of us."

Lauren squeezed Jason's arm with her hand. "Sorry, I'll be back in a little bit."

As Lauren headed back through the house, Derek could hear her footsteps overhead. He looked up and followed the movement of her steps with his eyes.

"Take him outside, but not for too long!" Lauren shouted from somewhere inside the house. Derek assumed she was probably near their front door. "It's still wet out there and I swear I heard him coughing last night!"

Derek's eyes widened. How could he hear Lauren so well when she was inside, he wondered? He couldn't make out anything the couple had said when they spoke to each other in that part of the house earlier. Derek took in his surroundings more carefully now. The walls of the crawl space were the same muted, gray brick of the home's exterior. The dirt floor on which he stood was covered with a thick, black tarp. Lawn equipment, storage bins, and dusty, long-discarded pieces of furniture weaved all around the tall concrete pillars of the home's foundation.

Outside, Jason made his way down the deck stairs with the baby. Derek's head jerked back in astonishment as he saw Jason's feet pass by an opening in the brick wall in front of him. The approximately one by one-half foot rectangular opening in the wall was a screened-in air vent that allowed air to circulate under the home during the warm summer months. Derek looked around and saw light filtering in through maybe a dozen or so of these air vents in the walls around him. *This is how I can hear them so well!* The crawl space air vents acted like little, open windows for Derek. When the couple burned their bacon, they had opened *their* windows—windows that couldn't have been more than a few feet above the air vent Derek was currently standing by. The two openings were close enough that with nothing to separate them, he could hear their voices perfectly.

Derek felt excitement build in his belly. *Hadn't Jason said it was going to be nice out? Something about leaving the windows open all week?* As long as the family spoke somewhere near an open window, Derek could move to whichever air-vent was positioned underneath and listen to them. But could he see them if they were outside? Derek moved closer to the vent that he had just seen Jason pass by. It was perfectly eye level. Derek leaned his head forward and peered into the backyard. Through the mesh-covered opening, Derek was able to see quite well. Jason was carrying Landon toward the very edge of the property. He was a tall, strong-looking man with broad shoulders and dark chocolate skin. His jet-black hair was kept neat and short. Wearing a bluish-gray T-shirt with matching checkered pajama bottoms, Jason looked every bit the part of the "morning dad." The child, Landon, seemed to be the perfect mix of his parents. Derek flashed back to the memory of the woman he had seen through the home's front window the night before. He remembered her having fair skin and lighter hair. Landon's skin tone seemed to fall somewhere between the two of them and his wild curly hair was the color of wet sand.

Derek guessed the child to be five or six months old. They had their backs to him now, and Jason was pointing at things high up in the trees for Landon to look at.

Derek continued to study the man from the mesh crawl space opening and noticed his arms were very muscular. Normally, he would find someone with Jason's kind of build intimidating—frightening even—but there was such softness in the way he cradled his son against his own body that it made Derek's throat tighten. His own father had never touched him in any way other than with anger. Derek didn't have many memories of him. And the memories he did have, he wished he didn't. Thankfully, Derek's father wasn't around very often or for very long. The last time he saw him, Derek was seven years old.

"Where is it, Angela?!" His father's voice ripped through their tiny trailer like lightening. "Goddamn it, Angela! I *said*, where the hell's it at?"

Derek's father, Mark, dumped the entire contents of their silverware drawer onto the kitchen floor. The forks, knives, and spoons clanged together with a grinding metal dissonance as they fell. Derek sat cross-legged in front of the television in the adjoining living room. He looked down at the little baggie he was hiding in his hand. Tightening his grip around the bag, Derek leaned forward and turned up the volume of his cartoons.

Derek's mother may have had her moods, but Mark's

baseline was volatile. Derek had learned the best thing to do when he got like this was just to stay out of his way. Angela came out of the bedroom, a laundry basket full of clothes on her hip. She unconsciously shuddered as she saw the mess of silverware on the floor. "Where's *what* at?"

Mark glanced over at Derek. "You know what I'm talking about," he hissed.

Angela rolled her eyes. "Please, like he doesn't know. You spend more time passed out in that goddamn bathroom than you do with him."

"Don't go getting all high and mighty on me. You ain't no better."

"I only smoke stuff!" she snorted. "And it's not like I do it that much anyway—only when I have to stay up."

Her signature low-slung ponytail swung out to the side of her face as she pushed the laundry basket forward with her hip. "Shit, can you blame me? Having you here's like taking care of two kids."

Mark kicked at the silverware on the ground.

"You don't work. I'm the only one in this goddamn house who's got a job. You don't know what that's like. A man's gotta have a break once in a while. That's all I want, a goddamn break. I guess that's askin' too much, isn't it?"

"Like I don't want a break?" Angela fired back. "I do all the cooking and cleaning and taking care of the kid around here. I don't get any freakin' breaks."

Derek's mom was no weakling. He admired that about her. She could give it back just as good as anyone could dish it out. Mark balled his hands into fists and moved closer to his wife. His blond hair was buzzed so short that it highlighted every divot in his pockmarked skin. Mark wasn't very big. He and Angela were pretty evenly matched heightwise, but the simple fact that he was a man gave him the physical advantage he needed. Angela eyeballed him now, weighing the risks.

"I'm gonna ask you this one more time," he said. "And you better gimme the right answer." His voice was now slow and controlled. "It was on the box on top of the toilet this morning. And now it's gone. Where did it go, Angela?"

The air left the room as she stepped forward. "You check your arm?"

Mark's eyes widened, but Angela held her ground.

Derek felt his body start to fold in on itself. His tiny fist tightened around the bag he was hiding. He tried to focus on the cartoons in front of him, but the characters on the screen started to bleed together into a wild mash-up of colors. A low chuckle began to brew deep inside of Mark's chest.

"You're funny," he said quietly. "You're *really* funny, you know that?"

Mark smiled a wide smile and shook his head back and forth, the chuckle rumbling like thunder inside of him. Derek listened to the laughter grow like some kind of grotesque beast. It snaked through Mark's body from his chest, into his nose, and then up into his throat where he was no longer able to contain it and had to open his mouth to let it out. His whole body shook with laughter. It surged through him in great big waves that finally crested with a few big snorts and chokes that had him bending forward to hold onto his knees for support. With his back hunched over, Mark turned his head toward Derek.

"Your mom's a regular riot, ain't she boy?" He was hardly able to catch his breath. At first, Derek thought he sounded genuinely amused. Derek felt his lips curl up into little a smile and nodded. He'd never seen his father laugh so much before. It was kind of funny. He giggled a little and felt a sense of relief wash over him, but as he looked over at his mother, Derek saw that she wasn't laughing. Angela stood frozen in place. There was a look of caution in her eyes that immediately silenced him. Mark watched as the smile faded from his son's face. He followed his eyeline to Angela.

"Why ain't you laughin'?" Mark straightened up and swung his leg out dangerously in Angela's direction. The two now directly faced one another. "Your son thinks it's funny."

Angela said nothing. Mark rubbed at the stubble on his chin. "'Least *he* has a sense of humor."

As his parents faced each other in silence, Derek thought he saw a brief flicker of something in his mother's eyes. Then, in what seemed like an instant, she threw down the basket of clothes that were on her hip and bolted for the front door. In one sweeping movement, Mark reached out and grabbed her by her ponytail. Her head snapped back like a rag doll.

"How funny are you now?!" he screamed as he threw her down to the ground.

Derek shut his eyes and covered his ears. He pressed his hands against his head so hard it hurt, but no matter how hard he tried, Derek couldn't keep the sounds out. He thought of his cartoons, of a mouse hitting a cat with a frying pan, of a bird running off the side of a mountain and hanging in mid-air before plummeting back down to the earth in one gigantic puff of smoke. In his mind's eye, Derek pictured a silly duck tied to some train tracks, waiting to be rescued. He saw the train hit its brakes as it came upon the duck. The brakes made this horrible, high-pitched screeching sound as the train slowed to a stop. Derek rocked back and forth. The sound of the brakes became louder and louder. He tried to change the picture in his brain, he tried to shut it out, but he couldn't stop it. He couldn't stop the train.

Derek felt something pull at his arms. It yanked him so hard that his butt lifted right off the carpet. Derek's fists were pressed so firmly against his ears that it took all of his father's strength to pry them off. With his hands taken off his ears, Derek was shocked to discover the dreadful squeal of the train wasn't in his head—it was in the room with him. But the hideous noise wasn't coming from a train. It was coming from him. He was screaming.

"Stop that!" Mark yelled. "I said stop it!" Derek understood what his father was saying, but he couldn't control it. Bloodcurdling, agonizing screams exploded out of his tiny body. They were awful high-pitched wails, like the cries of a wounded animal caught in a trap. Mark shook his son roughly by his shoulders. As he did, Derek's hands fell open by his sides and the bag he had been clutching tightly fell onto the ground next to him.

"So you're the joker?" Mark snatched the bag off the ground and hit Derek hard across the face. Derek's screams stopped. "What's wrong with you?"

Mark took a step back from his son in a strange mixture of fear and confusion. He was sweating and had a large angry gash that spread across the entire length of his forehead—a sign that Angela had not gone down entirely without a fight. A thin line of blood streamed down over Mark's eyebrow and into his eye. He wiped at the blood with the bottom of his shirt. As he pulled the shirt away, the white material turned a violent crimson color. "You're just as crazy as your damn mom."

Angela began lifting herself off the floor. "Get out of my house," she growled.

"Think I wanna stay here with you two crazy idiots?" Mark was still pissed off, but there was nervousness in his voice now. He stuffed the baggie into his pocket and hurried over to the door.

"Get out of my damn house and don't you ever come back!" Angela bellowed.

"You two deserve each other!" Mark said, taking a quick moment to look back over his shoulder. His eyes locked on Derek. "Good luck with your bitch of a mom," he said. "Kid don't even look like me."

That was it. That was the last time Derek saw his father. He never asked Angela where he was. He was curious, sure, but frankly, he was too scared she might actually know—even worse, that she might take him there.

Derek hadn't thought about that day in a long time. In fact, he was so lost in the memory now that he didn't see Jason walking back to the house with Landon until it was too late. They came to a stop right in front of where he was standing in the crawl space. Jason hoisted the baby up on his side, licked his thumb, and rubbed at something on the child's face. The two couldn't have been more than a few feet from Derek; all they had to do was look to the right and they would have come eye to eye with him through the wire mesh of the crawl space vent.

Derek held his breath but felt a strong tickle creep into the back of his throat as he did. There was no mistaking the feeling—he needed to cough. He knew he couldn't make the slightest bit of noise without alerting them to his presence, so he held it in. His whole body jerked and convulsed at the force it took to do so. If Jason hadn't been so caught up in looking at his own son, surely he would have noticed. As the two made their way back up the steps into the home, Derek's mother sidled up next to him in the crawl space.

"I know what you're thinking," she whispered in his ear with a smile. "But they don't know what you did."

Chapter 3

Lauren sat alone on the park bench staring at the blue-berry muffin laying in the sandy soil in front of her. It was early in the day and the park was empty. Even though the park was obviously constructed for children—with its playground equipment, swings, and bright wooden animal cut-outs poking in and out of the trees—it was one of Lauren's favorite places to come alone. The park was convenient, situated right down the street from their house. It also had a magical quality about it. She used to come to the park before she was pregnant and daydream about what it would be like to visit with her own child. Lauren smirked at the memory of those fantasies as she pulled a secret stash of cigarettes out of her purse. A little brown bird fluttered by as she plucked a cigarette from its pack and lit up. The bird landed next to her muffin on the ground. It peered up at Lauren apprehensively.

"Go ahead. One of us needs to eat."

The bird cocked its head to the side, almost as if it understood. Lauren smiled as she exhaled. "Don't tell on me, okay? Haven't had one of these things in two years."

Lauren closed her eyes as she took another deep inhale of her cigarette. She felt certain a sense of peace was only a drag or two away.

"Race ya!"

Lauren's body jerked forward as two boys zoomed past her, stealing her Zen and taking it along to the playground equipment with them. The boys were maybe around eight years of age or so. Based on the striking similarity between the two, Lauren guessed they were brothers.

"You really shouldn't smoke here."

Lauren turned around and saw a stubby, middle-aged woman walking up behind her. The woman was heavy. Wisps of her short, reddish, painfully out-of-date hair were just starting to cling to the fresh beads of sweat forming along her hairline. Her face was flushed and she was already huffing and puffing from her short walk over from the playground's parking lot.

"It's a playground," the woman said with disgust. "You shouldn't smoke here." Although she was short, the woman managed to look down her nose expertly at Lauren who began to feel heat rise in her cheeks.

"There are kids here," the woman continued, as if Lauren failed to grasp the point.

"I hear you," Lauren mumbled as she stood up. She felt

her hands start to shake as she pulled her purse strap over her shoulder.

"What?" the woman asked.

Lauren started to walk away. "I said, I hear you."

"Maybe when you have kids, you'll underst --"

In an instant, Lauren spun back around on her heels and flicked her still lit cigarette in the woman's face. "Maybe *you* can stop jamming cheeseburgers in your fat face, so you'll be able to play on the equipment with your kids instead of dying of a heart attack on the walk over to it!"

The woman jumped back. She brought her hands up in front of her body defensively, as if Lauren might strike her. Lauren glanced over at the boys who were on the playground. They sat on top of the monkey bars frozen, staring at her.

"Fun having someone point out your faults, isn't it? Makes you feel really good, doesn't it?"

The woman had no idea how to respond. Her mouth hung open and she shook her head back and forth with wide eyes. Lauren flashed the woman and her children a big, phony smile before turning to go. She could feel the woman's eyes follow her the entire walk back to her car. When she finally reached the parking lot, without looking back, Lauren threw her hand up in a dismissive wave and called out, "Have a great fucking day."

Lauren burst through the front door of the house with renewed manic energy. Grocery bags lined her arms and in her hands, she held a plastic six-pack container of muffins that was missing one muffin. Jason looked up from where he was cleaning some pans in the kitchen sink. "Hey, in the kitchen!"

On her way into the kitchen, Lauren stopped in front of Landon, who was happily playing inside of a rainbow-colored playpen. Jason had placed the playpen between the living room and kitchen, where he could keep a watchful eye on his son while cleaning up.

"How's my handsome little man?" Lauren cooed. "You look so handsome this morning. Yes, you do!"

"What's all this?" Jason interrupted, nodding at all the bags on his wife's arms.

Lauren noticed a box of pancake mix on the counter next to where her husband was doing dishes. "Did you guys eat already?"

"Yeah, we thought you got lost."

"Sorry." Moving into the kitchen, Lauren sighed as she put her bags down on the counter. "Store was crazy. Here, help me put these away, will ya? We need to head back out."

"Wait, back up a second. What *is* all this stuff?"

Lauren pulled a package of raw hamburger patties out from one of the bags. "Matt and Jessie are coming over this afternoon, remember?"

"Oh man, I forgot about that. So what, we're cooking?"

"I'm no expert, but yeah. I think that's usually what happens when you invite people over for dinner."

"Smart ass." Jason gave his wife a sideways smile.

"Come on. Help me," Lauren said.

"It'll be nice to have people over." Jason wiped his hands on a kitchen towel, flung the towel over his shoulder, and started helping his wife sort out the pile of groceries. "We haven't had anyone over since..." Jason stopped mid-thought. He cleared his throat and started again, "So what? Did you forget something?"

"No, why?"

"Because you said we needed to go back out."

"Mmmm, hang on." Lauren popped some apples in the fridge, closed the refrigerator door then pulled her cellphone out from her back pocket. "I have a list."

"Oh god, not a list." Jason hung his head. Lauren raised an eyebrow flirtatiously as she searched for the list she had saved on her phone.

Beneath the couple, Lauren had no idea Derek was able to hear them talking so well that he felt as though he were right there in the room with them. Looking up at the dusty ceiling of the crawl space, Derek tried to position himself right below where he imagined they were above him.

"Got the hamburger stuff already," Lauren said gleefully, swiping the item off of her digital list. She'd always loved her lists. She was as type-A personality as they came. Her lists gave her a sense of control—something she had come to appreciate over the last five months. "We need to drop the dry cleaning off, go to the car wash, get a costume for Landon..."

"I ordered one already," Jason said.

"You did?"

"Yup. World's smallest pirate hat, on its way."

"Well, is it going to be here on time?"

"Not my first rodeo."

"When did you order it? Halloween's *this* week. You know that, right?"

"Just mark it off the list. It's done." Jason reached for Lauren's phone, but she pulled it back. "What else you got?"

Lauren eyed her husband, deciding to let her anxiety over the costume pass. "Area rugs."

"Rugs?"

Under Lauren's feet, Derek moved his mouth and body, miming their conversation as it took place.

"Yeah, for the living room," Lauren said. "It's time."

"Time for...?"

Lauren motioned exasperatedly toward the rug in the living room. "Seriously? Look at it!"

Jason stared, blinking at their lovely living room.

"Look at the egg," Lauren prompted.

The beautiful, ornate Fabergé-esque egg that Lauren kept so carefully displayed on their fireplace mantle sat in its gold stand, at its perfect angle, as it always did. Jason stared at the egg, utterly confused. "I thought I was supposed to be looking at the rug?"

"That egg is the nicest thing we have in this whole house and that rug is from your old college apartment. The egg is a focal point. We should show it off!"

"Babe…"

"It's time to grow up, Jason. Why have anything nice if everything else is gonna look like crap?"

"I'm not arguing that it's not an old rug, or that we can't start getting nicer things," Jason groaned. "I'm just saying, we don't have to do everything right this second."

Jason knew that once she got something stuck in her head, there was no point in even trying to talk her out of it. Even still, he uttered one final protest. "It's Sunday."

Lauren's footsteps stomped across the floorboards above Derek. She slammed the cupboards as she put away the rest of the groceries.

"Exactly! When else will we have the time? I just got back to work. You know how crazy it's been trying to catch up on everything I've missed. You have your review this week. I have a counseling appointment Friday."

"Fine."

"Plus, there's a new pre-school teacher starting Tuesday, so, somehow I have to find time to go meet her 'cause I'm not having anyone watch Landon that I haven't checked…"

"I said fine, Lauren!"

The exasperated look on her husband's face made Lauren

feel immediately guilty. She had been moody before everything had happened, but Jason navigated these more intense, lingering fits of rage with an ease and calmness she would never be able to offer him should he ever need it.

Lauren stopped what she was doing and faced her husband in the kitchen. It was almost undetectable, but her voice trembled ever so slightly with a rare vulnerability. "I just want everything to be nice."

Their road may have been bumpier as of late, but Lauren knew that Jason loved her beyond reason. She could see it now as he stared deeply into her wide, almond-shaped eyes.

"Come here," Jason moved closer to his wife and gave her a kiss. It was a short kiss, but one filled with a long history. "I love you."

Unbeknown to Lauren, as the two of them pulled apart, Derek was imagining himself standing right there behind them.

"Lemme pack a bag for Landon," Jason said. "Then we'll go and look at these rugs of yours, okay?"

Lauren nodded and bit her bottom lip. She didn't deserve him.

In the crawl space, under the home, Derek suddenly became more aware of the old, discarded items from the Scotts' home that surrounded him. Derek walked over to one such item, a wooden bookcase. Reaching out to touch it, his finger left a deep mahogany trail in the thick dust that covered its shelves. Derek pulled his hand back to inspect the dust on his finger as the couple rustled around above. For the next twenty minutes or so, as the couple prepared to leave for their shopping trip, he stayed by the bookcase—thinking.

At one point, Derek heard Lauren call out, "You want me to close the windows and lock up?"

"Nah!" Jason answered, shouting back to her from the other side of the house. "We're not gonna be gone that long. It's safe."

Jason's voice returned to a normal volume as he moved back into the kitchen. "Besides, we gotta air this place out. I don't want it to smell like burned bacon when Matt and Jessie get here."

There were more steps and movements overhead, then Derek heard the sound of a door slam. His head jerked up and over toward the other end of the house as he recognized the familiar squeal of the Scotts' garage door opening. *They're leaving?* The silence that followed the squealing garage door suggested the family was now indeed gone. But, just to be sure they were, Derek waited a few more minutes before making his move. He squinted as he pushed the door of the crawl space open. After being in the dark for so long, the sounds of the outdoors seemed amplified and the sun's light seemed intensely new. The brightness of the sunshine overwhelmed him and he found that he had to lean against the side of the home for support for a moment.

In front of him, in the shade under the deck, Derek could

make out two red, plastic recycling bins lying on the ground. Next to the bins stood a large, bright green plastic trash can with black rubber wheels at its base and a flip-top lid. Derek remembered the burned bacon Jason had thrown out earlier and his stomach seized with an overwhelming hunger. He couldn't recall the last time he had eaten. The need for food—the need for anything really—hadn't occurred to him in quite some time. His body shook with a sudden anticipation as he made his way under the deck and opened the lid to the trash can. There was the bacon. It was lying right on top of an assortment of plastic rubbish and paper bags of varying sizes. Derek reached in and popped a piece of the bacon into his mouth. The salty, burned meat seemed to dance on his tongue. He felt some of the dizziness he had been suffering from begin to lift almost immediately. As he continued to pluck the bacon up and put it in his mouth with one hand, his other hand worked to search through the rest of the trash.

What he found in the trash was astonishing. Derek had never seen such waste! Hidden almost like Easter eggs throughout the trash can was a treasure trove of fresh food. He found chocolates, fruit, half of a roasted chicken still in its plastic store container, and a box of powdered doughnuts. The fresh food items were all placed, almost strategically, under or beside the regular-sized garbage bags in the trash can. He grabbed what appeared to be a used, paper lunch sack and began loading it up with a little bit of everything. He felt elated—it was almost like eating at a buffet! When he was done filling his sack, he closed the lid.

As he turned around to take his haul back into the crawl space, a white, fluffy cat darted out in front of him. The cat ran up the stairs to the deck and took a seat—almost politely—outside of the back door of the Scotts' home. Curious of the feline, Derek placed his bag of food down on the ground and wiped his mouth. He took a quick look around him. Once he was sure no one was watching, he cautiously made his way up the steps after the cat.

When he got to the top of the stairs, he stopped at the back door and stared in disbelief. The door had a large window in the center of it. The way the morning light hit the glass, the door had almost the same reflective quality as a mirror. Looking back at him from the shiny glass windowpane was a person Derek didn't recognize. This stranger was much taller than he remembered being. He was very pale, very dirty, and unbelievably thin. Although he was only fifteen, the gauntness lent an almost ageless quality to Derek's face; he could be a child or he could be thirty. He'd always thought of himself as a kid, but for the first time in his life, Derek actually thought he looked like a man. He took a step closer. He stared through his reflection to focus in on the couple's living room. The floors inside were a light-colored wood and the walls a cheery yellow. There was a large, fairly worn ornate area rug in the center of the room full of deep reds and blues. They had rich brown leather furniture. Pushed up against the wall, almost out of eyesight, stood a massive wooden entertainment center that housed an equally impressive flat screen television.

Derek pressed his face to the glass and turned his head to inspect the kitchen to his right. Closest to him was a large rectangular dining table. It was a deep cherry color—the same color as the tall cabinets in the kitchen behind it. One of six chairs around the dining table was pulled out a bit. Attached to the chair was a cream-colored booster seat. Derek imagined the baby, Landon, sitting in the chair.

The buttery color of the kitchen's granite countertops further added to the warmth of the home. Although everything inside was clean and had its own "place", the house had a cozy, lived-in look that to Derek, made it almost seem to glow.

"Fancy people."

Derek swung around toward the sound of his mother's voice coming from behind him, but all he saw was the white cat scurrying down the stairs into the yard. He turned back to the window, but instead of standing outside of the Scotts' home, he found he was now standing outside of his and his mother's trailer home.

He had lived in this same tiny trailer his entire life. It wasn't more than ten miles from Lauren and Jason's house, but in terms of lifestyle, the two seemed a million miles apart. Whereas Jason and Lauren's home was nestled in a quiet, upscale community, Derek's home was extremely isolated. He and his mother lived in a mobile home situated all alone at the end of a long dirt road, just outside of a large trailer park community. They weren't part of that community—they weren't part of anything. His mom owned their trailer outright, which she had some kind of strange, angry entitlement about. He knew that the trailer had been given to her by someone in her family, but the circumstances surrounding how she had actually acquired it remained closely guarded. "It's the least they could have given me," she'd say from time to time. "They owed me a hell of lot more than this for what they did." He didn't know what that meant.

His mother never talked about family. Derek could only remember one time when he'd dared to even ask her about it. That's what he was seeing now. As he looked through the window at what had just been the Scotts' beautiful kitchen, Derek saw his mother drinking coffee at their kitchen table. The table was now a cheap, white piece of plastic outdoor furniture with two folding metal lawn chairs beneath it. A cigarette had burned down, long forgotten, in the ashtray next to her.

Derek saw himself as he'd been in the fourth grade, approaching her at the table. His teacher had given him a history assignment. Everyone in class was asked to do a research paper on a living relative; the one stipulation being the paper couldn't be done on one's own mother or father.

"Ma'am?"

Angela was deep into one of her crossword puzzles. She

loved any kind of game involving words. They must have had at least fifty or sixty books of them stacked neatly into piles around their trailer. She hated clutter, but for her puzzles, she could make the exception.

"Ma'am?" Derek said a little louder this time.

His mother lifted only her eyes to Derek, but she wasn't there, even though she was looking right at him. Derek wondered if she could even see him. It took a few moments for the fog to clear and when she spoke, her voice was flat.

"I'm busy," she said.

"I know, ma'am. It's just..." Derek fumbled to find the right words. "It's just that...I need some help with something for school. I'm supposed to write a paper about someone in our family, not you, though." Derek stopped, unsure of how to finish, then added, "It's due tomorrow, ma'am."

His mother stared at him, expressionless. She blinked a couple of times and then slowly lowered her book onto the table.

"What do you want to know?" Her voice was ice cold. It made a nervous lump rise in Derek's throat.

"Ummm...I dunno," he said. "Do we have a family? I mean, *is* there someone I can write about?"

His mother drummed her fingers on the table a few times then fished a cigarette and lighter out of the small pocket of her T-shirt.

"Someone you can write about," Angela repeated acrimoniously. She lit the cigarette, took a drag, and leaned back in her chair.

"Well," she said after a moment of thought. "I guess you could write about your great aunt."

"I have a great aunt?"

"*Had* a great aunt," she corrected him. "She's dead now."

"Who was she?" Derek asked timidly.

"She was a nurse during World War II."

Derek's eyes widened.

"Oh yeah," his mom said. "She was a looker, too. A lot of powerful men wanted to marry that one."

"What was her name?" Derek asked.

"Her name? Let's see..." Deep wrinkles spread across Angela's forehead as she scrunched her eyebrows together. "I think her name was Lorraine. Yeah, that's it. Lorraine."

"Wait a second, ma'am!" Derek ran into the living room. He grabbed a pencil and notepad out of his backpack and then hurried back to the kitchen filled with excitement. "I want to get this all down!"

Angela smirked as her son threw himself down in the chair across from her and started writing.

"So her name was Lorraine," Derek repeated. "And she was a beautiful nurse—during which war?"

"World War II," she said.

His mother leaned forward to look down at what he was writing. "Yeah, you can put in there that she was quite a woman—a hero actually. She saved the lives of many of America's greatest men."

When Derek looked up, his eyes were wide and full of stars. "Really?" he breathed.

His mom took another drag of her cigarette. As she blew the smoke out, she stood up from the table.

"No," she said, stubbing out the cigarette in the ashtray. "I made that shit up. And that's exactly what you're going to do."

Derek's face fell.

"We have no family," she snapped. "They're all dead. And they would'na been worth writing about when they were alive neither."

His mother was visibly agitated. "What's wrong with that school of yours? What makes them think they have any right to pry into people's private business, huh?"

Derek shook his head. His mother snatched her purse off the kitchen counter. She huffed off toward the front door, but as her hand touched the knob, she froze. She slowly turned around to face him. "Who asked you to write this paper, anyway?"

Derek shrugged, "Misses Taylor."

His mom stared him down. "And did everyone get asked to write a paper?"

"Yes, ma'am. I think all of her classes have to do one."

"Huh." Her voice was filled with suspicion. His mother considered this for a moment and then threw the strap of her purse roughly over her shoulder. "Of course everyone has to do one," she said. "The only difference between us and them is that I know what they're doing." His mother wagged her finger at Derek. "I sure do. Boy, I know *exactly* what they're doing."

Angela turned back around and yanked the door open. "I need to get outta here. You make something up. If that bitch teacher of yours doesn't believe you, you tell her to call me. I'll set her straight." Angela paused. "You're lucky you have me, you know that?"

There was something sharp in his hand. Derek opened his fist and saw two little pieces of white, jagged plastic. He touched his finger to the objects and moved them curiously around in his palm. Both pieces were thick and curved on one end and then tapered down into a thinner broken rectangular shape on the other end. They looked like two little, white plastic candy canes whose red stripes had been stolen. Derek didn't know where the plastic pieces had come from, but whatever they were, they appeared to have been snapped off of something larger. Derek looked up. It was only then that he realized where he was. He was standing right in the middle of Jason and Lauren's dining room!

How did I get in here?! Derek stumbled backwards into the granite countertop of the kitchen's center island. The door to the back deck hung wide open in front of him. *Did I do that?* He had absolutely no recollection of doing so. The last thing he remembered was staring at his reflection in the windowpane of the back door. Not remembering that he opened the door frightened him. He wondered how long he had been inside.

Derek tried to piece together what had happened. He tried to remember, but the more he tried to focus, the more disorganized it all became. He started to cough. At first it was just a little, but the more he did, the more phlegm broke up in his chest, and he found himself dizzy and gasping for breath. Derek leaned back and gripped onto the counter behind him for support. His balance felt off. He tried to focus on the things in the home, but everything he looked at took on a distorted, fun house quality. How long had he been inside? What had he done? He could feel his heart beating hard in his chest. The walls of the home pulsated with the exact same rhythm ever so slightly—in and out, in and out, in and out. He could feel the sound like a bass drum beating in his stomach.

Derek took a step forward to leave the home, but he tripped over his own feet and fell to the floor. The walls in the house bulged inward. He cradled his head and watched terrified as the drywall around him ripped and stretched, holding back some ungodly, unseen force. The whole house had become a dam, the heavy rush of the unknown threatening to break at any moment. A high-pitched ringing filled the room. It was the sound of the train from the cartoons he watched as a child. Derek shook his head to try and stop it. When that didn't work, he began hitting himself in the head with the base of his hand. *What have I done? What have I done? What have I done?* His thoughts raced and zig-zagged in an unnerving, disjointed way that unfortunately was starting to become something of a regular occurrence for him. *Because germs have wiped out entire civilizations, so I need to meet Erika at...Ms. Wendy's. She would love to have lunch with us. She hates turkey sandwiches.*

"Stop!" he yelled at the walls. "Stop it!" He screamed. "Stooopppp!"

As if on command, as the very last "stop" escaped from his body, everything inside of him and inside of the house went still. Derek's head jerked back in astonishment. Had the house heard him? He could hear a pin drop in the home now. The silence was so heavy, it seemed loud. *Yes*, he thought. It must have heard him. What other explanation could there be? That was it! That was the secret of the house! It was alive! That's why he had been so drawn to it. Derek sat upright at the epiphany. It was alive, all right. It was alive and it had listened to him. It had challenged him, yes, but Derek instantly understood that it had been a test. How else could he explain the unearthly glow he'd seen around the home, the open crawl space, the food waiting for him in the trash can? He was invited here!

A small smile crossed his lips and he nodded a somewhat self-conscious "thank you" to the room as he lifted himself back onto his feet. He belonged here. He was welcome to stay. It was going to take care of him. As Derek stood there feeling buzzed, reveling in his accomplishment, he became aware of a stinging sensation in the palm of his hand. He opened his fist and again saw the two little pieces of white plastic. They had cut deeply into his skin during the test. He wiped the blood off on his shirt and went to place the pieces on the counter. As he did, the house began to rumble, disapprovingly. Derek instantly picked the pieces back up and tucked them into the pocket of his jeans. The rumbling stopped and the house illuminated with warm light.

Derek nodded, indicating he understood. He still had no idea what these plastic pieces were, but they were obviously a gift from the house—a gift with great power. He would be sure to take good care of them. Derek took one final look around the house—*his* house. *We'll have a chance to get better acquainted soon*, he thought, *but right now I have to get moving.* There was a lot of work to be done before his family got back.

Closing the back door of the home carefully behind him, Derek made his way back down to the crawl space. The white, fluffy cat was still waiting for him at the base of the stairs. While he had been inside, the cat had discovered the bag of food he'd taken from the trash and left on the ground earlier. Derek reached out to pet the cat as it licked and chewed at the corner of the bag. It was so soft!

"You hungry?"

Derek gently scooped the cat up into his arms. "Yeah, me too." *There's more than enough food for the both of us to share,* he thought happily. He'd always wanted a pet. Derek grabbed the bag full of food and took it and the cat into the crawl space with him.

Chapter 4

"Well, look at what the cat dragged in!" Jason called out. The laughter started the very moment Matt and Jessie walked through the door.

"Hey, buddy," Matt replied. He and Jason loosely shook hands and clapped each other on the back.

"Awww, the man hug. How cute," Lauren joked as she scooted around them to get to Jessie. "Come here, girl! Give me a real hug!"

The two women squealed with delight as they locked arms around one another. Matt and Jason looked at both women and then at each other. Not missing a beat, Jason grabbed Matt by the hands. "Come here, man!" He cried, poking fun at the girls. The two men jumped up and down in an overly dramatic display of affection. Jessie and Lauren met their husbands' impressions with blank stares.

"I think I prefer the man hug," Jessie said, dryly. "Hey, where's the baby?"

"Napping."

Lauren grabbed Jessie by the hand and pulled her friend into the kitchen. "Whaddya want to drink?"

All the commotion occurring above him—caused by the excitement of Matt and Jessie visiting—made Derek feel frantic. He took a step back and surveyed his work in the crawl space. The table seemed off. He thought it had been closer to the door. He reached down and moved the green storage bin a few inches closer to the wall, then stepped back and nodded approvingly. Two more empty storage bins were placed deliberately to his left, directly under where he remembered Jason and Lauren's living room sofa and coffee table were. Derek hurried over to where he heard Jason and Matt talking now and tried to get their placement a bit more accurate.

Derek had discovered a light in the crawl space—nothing fancy, just a crude light bulb screwed into the ceiling. When he pulled the long white string attached to the light fixture, the crawl space glowed warmly. He knew that it would be impossible to use the light in the evenings as the Scotts would surely notice a light shining under their home in the dark of night. But Derek had tested the light while the Scotts had been gone and found that it was virtually undetectable from outside during the bright daylight hours. With the light on, Derek was better able to take inventory of all the things around him: old bookcases, pictures, and storage bins. Not only did he have a ton of furnishings to work with, but the thick layer of dust on everything told Derek something very important—the couple never came down there.

In fact, it appeared the only items in the crawl space that had been used recently were a lawnmower and a wheelbarrow. Derek didn't worry about those things, though. It was October now and all of the grass and plants had gone dormant for the season. Derek felt confident Jason and Lauren would have no use for any lawn equipment anytime soon. Derek felt good; the cold he had been suffering from was starting to subside. He felt stronger, hopeful even. For the first time in a long time, Derek felt as though he had something to look forward to.

The white cat swirled around Derek's legs as he grabbed the bag of food he had fished out of the Scotts' trash earlier and brought it over to his makeshift dining table.

"I know," Derek whispered to the cat. "Not yet."

He knew how the cat felt. Derek was starving, too, but it would be rude to eat before everyone else sat down.

In the kitchen, Lauren poured a glass of wine for Jessie and then herself.

"Hold up. What is this monster?" she heard Matt ask Jason in the living room. Lauren instantly knew the "monster" Matt was referencing was Jason's mammoth, new flat screen television.

"Like that?" Jason asked. "Forty-two inches."

Matt whistled, like he was impressed. "Plasma?"

"No, LED."

Lauren craned her head back to see into the living room. She saw Jason grab a remote off of the coffee table and turn on the television.

"Check out the picture on this thing," Jason said.

"Nice, man"

"Hang on." The excitement in Jason's voice mounted as he picked up another remote. "Let me turn on the sound bar, so you get the full affect."

Lauren turned to her friend seeing that the guys had become absorbed in the other room. She held her index finger up to her lips, letting Jessie know to stay quiet. Lauren raised her shirt revealing a lighter and joint tucked into the waistband of her jeans—Jessie's mouth fell open. Lauren jerked her shirt back down and nodded her head toward the backyard.

"Ummm, hey Lauren, it's so nice out," Jessie said, responding to her friend's cue in a hilarious "bad acting" voice. "Why don't you take me outside and show me those new bushes you guys planted?"

Derek startled as he heard the girls bound out of the kitchen and onto the back deck.

"Hey, where are you two going?" Derek heard Jason call out after the women from inside.

"Back in a sec!" Jessie yelled back.

"Girl talk!" Lauren added slamming the door shut behind them before Jason could ask anything more.

The two women ran down the back steps, giggling like school children. Derek leaned over quickly to pick up the cat that had planted itself next to his feet. He stood very still in the crawl space with the animal in his arms as he listened to the women dip around the side of the house. Derek looked at the brick walls, following their voices with his eyes.

As the two women huddled against the side of the house, Lauren pulled the joint and lighter out of her waistband.

"I haven't done this in forever," Jessie gushed. "Do you think anyone can see us?"

"Maybe some squirrels," Lauren joked, nodding at the forest that circled their home.

Jessie touched a low-hanging tree branch. "Yeah, but the woods aren't that thick. Think your neighbors are gonna smell it?"

"Oh my god, chill out." Lauren lit up and inhaled deeply.

"Where'd you get it?" Jessie asked.

"Heather," Lauren coughed as she breathed out a cloud of smoke.

"The girl you do yoga with? What a cliché."

"Nah, she's cool. We're friends." Lauren handed the joint off to Jessie, who eagerly accepted. "Everyone has their own idea of how to 'help' me, ya know? I have to say, I think her approach has been the best so far."

From inside the crawl space, Derek noticed smoke wafting in through one of the air vents near where the women were standing. He immediately recognized the distinctly sweet smell.

"I feel like we're back in high school," Derek heard Lauren say.

"Yeah, only we're not huddled over a toilet in a dirty bathroom stall. Though it does kinda smell like piss out here. What the…?"

Derek heard Lauren sniff the air. "It does," she agreed. "It's probably the neighbor's stupid cat, Mr. Fluffy. Don't tell Jason. He hates that thing."

Derek glanced down at Mr. Fluffy, who was happily purring away in his arms.

"Mr. Fluffy? For real? That's its name? Ugh, the smell's really strong. Sure that's a cat and not a bear or something?"

Lauren chuckled at her friend. Jessie's beautiful red hair was swept up into a bun and even though she used make-up to cover them up, her matching red freckles were still visible under the bright fall sunshine. Lauren thought about how she'd watched those freckles change shape and color over the years. She could probably draw the exact placement of each one on a piece of paper by memory. Jessie was the first person she'd met when her parents had moved from Maryland to Alabama when she was just a kid. They grew up on the same block, even went to high school and college together. Lauren knew they'd probably still be living on the same block if it hadn't been for the great job her husband had been offered a couple years back.

"I wish you lived closer," Lauren sighed.

"Me too." Jessie passed the joint back to Lauren. She rested her back against the side of the house as she blew out the smoke. "It's only a two-hour drive, though. Besides, we'd get into way too much trouble if we lived next to each other."

Lauren lifted the joint in front of her face. "Point taken."

On the other side of the wall, Derek began to move toward the women, ever so slowly, conscious of the noise created by every tendon, every muscle and bone in his body. When he reached the other side of the wall where the women stood together, he carefully placed Mr. Fluffy on the ground. Derek realized the women weren't speaking anymore, and began to fear that the women had heard him, when Jessie finally broke the awkward silence.

"So, you look good," he heard her say.

"Oh god, don't do that. Please don't do that," Lauren groaned.

"Do what?"

"Don't act like you don't know how to act around me. We've been friends since we were five, Jessie."

"I *don't* know how to act! I've never gone through this with someone before…"

"I'm the same person, Jess. So bringing home my baby wasn't exactly the dream social media post. I feel like crap about that. Think I need to be reminded of it every single day?"

"No, I'm…"

"Postpartum's pretty common, ya know. And it's almost over. I got help, right away, like you're supposed to. It's almost over."

"Sorry! I'm trying…I'm not…" Jessie sighed in defeat. "I'm trying, Lo. I didn't know I wasn't allowed to ask how you were doing."

"Of course you can ask how I'm doing!"

"How are you doing?"

"Well, if you must know, I'm snapping at people a lot!"

Derek stared at the brick wall wide-eyed as the girls paused in conversation again. The absolute absurdity of the moment hit them both at the exact same moment. Laughter mixed with tears as the two women embraced.

"Oh my god, I love you," Jessie gushed. "You know I love you."

"I love you, too. I'm sorry," Lauren said, burying her head in her friend's shoulder. "I'm such a freak show right now."

Lauren couldn't feel it, but behind her Derek tenderly reached out a hand to touch the wall she was standing against. He imagined what Lauren looked like on the other side: puffy red face, snotty nose. He pictured the wall dissolving between the two of them. He imagined his fingers were touching Lauren's shoulder, not the wall.

"A *total* freak show," Jessie agreed. "But you're *my* freak show, girl."

Lauren giggled against Jessie's soft, cotton shirt.

"I'm good. I am," Lauren said. She reluctantly let go of her friend and wiped at her face. "Besides the guilt thing, I'm fine. But that's normal from what the counselor tells me. I'm sleeping again. Jason's been great—really patient. I'm not really into sex yet, which is annoying the crap out of him."

"That's not postpartum. That's called marriage, honey."

Lauren laughed. Jessie had this breezy, beautiful way about her that made everything just seem easier.

Jason's voice called from the backyard. "Where are you?"

Lauren jerked forward at the sound of her husband's voice. Derek jerked back at the same time, the wall suddenly reappearing between the two of them.

"Be right there!" He heard the girls call back in unison.

Derek placed his hands on the wall in front of him, devastated. He closed his eyes and tried to will the wall away again, but the harsh texture of the brick remained.

"Gimme that," Jessie grabbed the joint from Lauren's hand and stubbed it out on the bottom of her shoe.

Lauren panicked. "Oh damn, he's totally going to be able to smell it on me."

Keeping the extinguished joint held tightly between her fingers, Jessie used her other free hand to begin frantically fanning Lauren.

"What are you doing?'

"Waving the smell off of you!"

"What?" Lauren swatted at her friend's hand. "Stop that. *You're* the freaking freak show!"

"There you are!" Jessie and Lauren both screamed in surprise as Jason came towards them from around the corner of the house. "What are you doing? The whole neighborhood can hear you two cackling," Jason said.

Jessie and Lauren broke out into the loud and uninhibited kind of laughter that can only be produced by friends who have known each other since childhood.

"You are so busted." Jason lifted his hands out to his sides. "Is there anything maybe you were going to tell me?"

Misreading his open hands, Jessie dutifully dropped the extinguished joint in Jason's palm.

"Wow. What? No. And thanks, I'll keep that. I was talking about the window."

Jessie and Lauren shot each other confused looks.

"Wait…you mean you didn't notice?" Jason asked.

"Notice what?" Lauren was careful not to incriminate herself any further.

"You broke the window."

Lauren, thankful for any distraction from her current impropriety, felt her confidence rushing back. "I most certainly *did not* break the window."

"Yeah, you did. Matt and I were just closing the windows to test the sound system and the one at the top of the stairs is broken."

"How loud were you going to turn it up that you felt you needed to close the windows?" Lauren asked.

"Don't try to change the subject. You're the one who opened all the windows this morning. *After* nearly burning down the kitchen, I might add."

"What do you mean it's broken?"

"The latches that keep it locked? They're broken clean off."

"What on earth?" Lauren rounded the corner of the house. "Let me see."

Jason and Jessie followed close behind.

Inside the crawl space, something clicked in Derek's head. He stuck his hand in his pocket and dug out the little white pieces of plastic that he had found in the home earlier.

"It shuts, so there's no rush to fix it," Derek heard Jason explain to the group as they gathered in the kitchen above him. "But it doesn't lock. See? You're the only one who opened it, Lauren."

Matt, who was probably trying to make Lauren feel better, said, "It's supposed to be gorgeous all week. You guys'll probably have the windows open every day anyway."

"What the hellll?" Lauren drew out the question, sounding utterly mystified. "How the heck did I manage to do that?"

Laughter broke out over Derek's head. He heard Lauren open and close the window several times, like a man who knows nothing about cars but looks under the hood anyway, somehow believing if he looks at the engine long enough, the problem might just fix itself. Deciding to leave the window open, Lauren turned to her friends and said, "Well, that's really weird. Help me look, guys."

"Look for what?" Jessie's voice and response time were both a bit delayed from the pot.

"The little latchey-thingey-mabobs."

"Is that the technical term?" Matt joked.

"We've already looked, babe," Jason said. "Besides, they're snapped clean in half. Even if we do find them, we can't put them back on."

"Shoot," Derek heard Lauren say. "But if the latches broke off, they should be here, right? Where else could they be?"

Below, Derek stared up into the floorboards on which Lauren stood above him. Lauren became still for a moment. He could almost feel her eyes staring back down at the floor towards him.

"Are you cold?" Jason asked.

"Huh?" Lauren looked up from the floor. "No. Why?"

"You're covered in goosebumps."

Lauren glanced down and saw all the hair on her arms sticking straight up. Before she could respond, Landon started wailing in the back bedroom.

"And guess who's up?" Lauren said, seeming to shake off a chill. "Perfect timing."

As everyone headed back to the bedroom to see the baby, Derek cupped the latches to the window in his hands. He brought them to his mouth and breathed out hard so that the little pieces rattled around like dice. Closing his fists, Derek brought them to his heart. They were a gift from the house. He could come and go now whenever he pleased. It was the best gift he had ever been given.

Chapter 5

Laughter wafted down to Derek out of the broken open window of the Scotts' dining room.

"I am NOT that bad!" Lauren slapped her hand down on the table next to her almost empty dinner plate.

Jason, who was sitting next to her, put an arm around his wife's chair. "You fixate," he said.

"You do kinda fixate," Jessie agreed from across the table.

"Give me an example," Lauren challenged.

"An example?"

"Yeah, an example."

"Just today!" Jason volunteered for Jessie. "Just today, you wanted to go look at rugs because you don't like how our current rug makes the egg look in the living room."

Lauren nodded, not denying the accusation. "I stand by that."

"What egg?" Matt asked, confused.

"There." Jessie pointed to the egg that sat on the fireplace mantle in the room next to them. "It's a Fabergé egg, right?"

Lauren cleared her throat. "Yes, well…"

"It's not even Russian!" Jason said, cutting her off. "It has 'Made in Italy' stamped on the bottom!"

"Okay, it's *like* a Fabergé egg. It's still expensive! That's twenty-four karat gold on there!"

"It's nice," Matt remarked.

"She got it at an estate sale," Jessie said, turning her body in her chair to face her husband who was sitting next to her. "We should really go to one of those."

"Forget the egg!" Jason's voice cut through the lively conversation. "Does anyone care about us not needing the rug?!"

"Hah!" Lauren cried out triumphantly. "See, I told you! It's a focal point!"

The couples both broke into fits of laughter.

In the dim crawl space, hidden away from the happy foursome above him, Derek had positioned his makeshift dining table directly below the couples. He sat on the ground. The food from the Scotts' trash can sat untouched on the table in front of him. He was hungry and wanted to eat, but an unexpected dinner guest was greatly affecting his appetite.

Angela sat quietly across from Derek. She drummed her fingers on the table, her eyes fixed on the ceiling above as the dinner party conversation raged on.

"No, I agree. Lists are important!" Derek heard Jessie say, coming to her friend's defense.

"Thank you!" Lauren replied, vindicated.

"Does Jessie make lists?" Jason asked Matt.

"Nah, Jess is pretty chill."

"I'm chill!" Lauren shrieked. "See, look!" It was quiet for a moment while Derek pictured Lauren giving her best impression of what she imagined "chill" to look like. Once again, the couples erupted in laughter. Derek was amused by their lively conversation. He had never been around people who laughed so much. He couldn't understand how any one person could be that happy, let alone a room full of people. Angela's reaction, however, was quite different. She cringed in disgust every time the laughter broke out above. "I don't like them," she growled. "They have no manners."

Derek knew her comments were, of course, directed at the lack of structure in the couples' conversations. Their voices were loud and often overlapped. They cut each other off. Angela had strict rules about that. You never talked out of turn in her home. She was big into rules and manners. While Derek was growing up, everything had to be done according to a specific schedule; everything had to have a purpose. Dinner in their home was very systematic. She seemed to get confused and angry if even the slightest thing was off.

"Remember when you made us late that one time?" Angela asked. Derek shuddered as a wide wolfish grin spread across his mother's face.

It was a warm September day. Derek sat on the curb outside of his school, his sack of books placed neatly next to his feet. Derek's backpack had a huge ripped hole in the bottom of it, and until his mother could get the money to buy a new one, Derek would have to carry his books in a plastic grocery bag. He was only a few weeks into his fourth grade year, and school had ended for the day. He had waited patiently, watching the buses fill with kids he'd never played with and then pull out of the parking lot one by one. When the teachers' cars started leaving the lot, Derek began to feel nervous. One of the teachers, a man he wasn't familiar with, rolled down his window as he passed and asked Derek if he was okay. Flashing a well-practiced smile, Derek lied, saying he knew his mom was running late and that she would be there any minute. The teacher gave Derek a concerned look and then glanced up at the sky. "You sure I can't give you a ride? It looks like it's going to start raining soon."

Derek reassured the teacher that he was all right, but the truth was, he *was* worried. It was completely out of character for his mom to be late. The air was humid. It started drizzling as the very last car pulled away from the school lot. It was almost five o'clock. Dinner at his house was always at six o'clock sharp—no exceptions. His mother would never do anything to jeopardize that. Where was she? He didn't want to move, but a growing pressure in his bladder had become too uncomfortable to ignore. With an uneasy stomach, Derek picked up his sack of books and made his way back toward the school. He pulled on the big silver handles to the main entrance, but the doors were locked. "Hello? Is anybody in there?"

Derek pressed his face to the long windows that were on each side of the metal doors and looked in. He hoped to see a janitor or someone who could let him in to use the restroom, but the school was completely dark. Slowly making his way around the side of the building, Derek tried other entrances but came to the same conclusion—all of the doors were locked. A sense of urgency set in that had him grabbing at his crotch and dancing back and forth on his tiptoes. He began to run. Derek knocked on every one of the low, rectangular classroom windows as he flew down the side of the long, one-story school. When he got about three quarters of the way down the building, he stopped. One of the windows had easily swung open when he hit it.

The window was just low enough for him to be able to reach and just large enough for him to fit through. Derek quickly looked to his left and right. The school backed up to some woods—nobody would be able to see him. He took a deep breath and pushed the window inward, but as he pulled himself up, the pressure of the wall against his bladder proved too much and the warm, yellow liquid began streaming down the inside of his pant legs. It was a heavy flow. Derek didn't even try to hold it back. He let his belly slump against the wall and breathed a deep sigh of relief as the urine coursed down his thighs and into his shoes. When he was finished, he rolled around so that his back rested against the building. He slid down the wall and took a seat on the ground. Derek took a minute to enjoy the sensation. It was heavenly.

He let his head fall forward, but as he did, his relief quickly turned to dread. The jeans he was wearing were a light denim wash and there was no mistaking what had happened. The material over his crotch had turned dark blue, three or four shades darker than it ought to have been. Derek jumped to his feet. Things were even worse than he'd feared. In addition to the soaked front of his jeans, there were also great big lines of dark blue that trickled all the way from the source down to his feet. Derek panicked. What would his mother think? Maybe she wasn't coming. Maybe they'd be dry by the time she got there. Could he take them off? Could he tell her they'd gotten wet in art class?

Before Derek could come up with a concrete plan, he heard the sound of a car horn coming from the front of the school. His heart started racing. There was no mistaking the high, off-key beep of his mom's car horn. The short, frenetic blasts of the horn were close together and Derek could feel the impatience in them as he grabbed his books and ran towards the front of the school. By the time he got there, she was laying on the horn. Even after she'd made eye contact with him, his mother continued to press down. Angela's eyes were wild and full of anger. She looked as though she was about to scream, but when Derek opened the passenger side door, she froze. Her eyes fixed on the wet spot on the front of his pants. Her lips curled back over her teeth in pure revulsion

"What...is...*that*?" She croaked, barely able to form the words.

Derek looked down, ashamed. His mother furiously began flapping her hands up and down in some unintelligible command.

"I got them wet," Derek's voice broke as tears welled up in his eyes.

"Take them off."

"What?"

"Take off your pants! Take them off!" she shrieked.

The sound of the horn had drawn the attention of an older gentleman who was walking his dog across the street. Alarmed by the screaming, the man jogged over, coming to a stop next to Derek.

"Is everything okay here?" he asked. The dog growled at Angela.

As if someone flipped a switch, her face immediately softened. "Get in the car, honey," she said to Derek. "You can grab that blanket off the back seat and sit on that, okay? Don't worry, we'll get ya all cleaned up when we get home."

Derek's eyes widened with surprise. He quickly jumped at her orders and grabbed the blanket out of the back. The man gave Angela a long, hard look.

"Kids," she laughed at the stranger. "They can drive you crazy sometimes, can't they?"

The man wasn't buying what she was selling and he didn't answer, but Angela continued to smile at the man as Derek climbed into the passenger seat next to her.

"Buckle your seatbelt, dear."

Derek could feel the man's eyes burning into him as he pulled the belt across his chest. He flashed the stranger his small practiced smile and the man nodded back.

Angela called out a cheerful, "Bye now!" to the man, but he didn't respond. Instead, the stranger gave his mother a cautious look and took a slow step back onto the curb. The man and his dog stayed rooted to the spot. They both eyed the car warily as it pulled away. His mother's eyes darted up to the rearview mirror several times, watching them. When Angela was sure her car was out of sight, she veered off onto a side street Derek wasn't familiar with. It was a construction site for new homes.

They pulled over in front of the entrance where a white sign poked out of the freshly scraped ground that read, "Who Says You Can't Have it All?" The site was empty for the day, but a great hulking bulldozer caught Derek's eye as their car came to a stop. The bulldozer was big, shiny and yellow, and the wheels on it were so high off the ground Derek imagined you'd have to have a ladder to be able to get on top of them. He turned to his mother to tell her so, but as he did, her arm swung forward, knocking him so hard across the face that his head flew back into the seat behind him and then bounced forward into the dashboard.

"Where were you?!" she screamed.

Derek brought his hands to his face and hunched his shoulders forward. She took off her seatbelt and began slapping his head and arms. "I was sitting outside of that damn school for ten minutes!"

When he didn't answer, she struck the back of his head with the palm of her hand. "Did you hear me? Where were you?"

When Derek failed to answer again, Angela leaned across him, opened the passenger side door, and unclicked his seat-belt. "Get out!"

His mother turned sideways in her seat and lifted her legs. "I said, get the hell out!" She screamed as she kicked him. Her legs were strong and she was easily able to push him out of the car. Derek fell into a heap on the dirt.

"How could you embarrass me like that? Don't you ever do that to me again, do you hear me?!"

No sooner had Angela slammed the passenger side door than the wheels of the car began to spin in place as she pressed down on the gas. Derek watched from the ground as the car skidded out and away from him. She hadn't gotten very far from him when Angela suddenly jerked the wheel and swung the car back around in his direction. The car kicked up dust as it headed straight for him. Derek's eyes widened in fear. She surely meant to kill him. At the last second, though, Angela turned the wheel. She hit the brakes and stopped dangerously close to Derek's terrified body on the ground. Angela rolled down the window.

"You're walking home," she hissed. "And when you get home, you throw out those piss-soaked baby pants, clean your sorry ass up, and go straight to bed. You touch anything," she warned, "you talk to anyone on the way home, I'll kill you. Do you hear me? I swear, I will kill you."

His mother spit near his crumpled body and then peeled out of the lot so fast it made Derek's head spin. He laid there for a few seconds until the initial shock of what had just happened wore off and then gradually got to his feet. His face was streaked with tears, dirt, and snot. He looked around, embarrassed, as he wiped his face with his hands.

Home was about five miles away and Derek estimated that if he kept up a good pace, it would take him until at least seven to get there. He lifted his chest high and steeled himself as he walked out of the construction site. *I won't feel sorry for myself*, he thought. *I won't*. But as he turned the corner onto the main road that would take him home, the sky opened up and his resolve quickly began to crumble. The raindrops felt extra cold against the burning heat in his face. Derek started to snif-fle as the traffic picked up. Droves of men and women were on their way home from a busy day at the office. Not one of them gave him a second glance.

His thoughts turned in circles as he walked on. Why hadn't he just run to the back of the building in the first place and peed on the wall? Why had he felt the need to go inside? None of this would have happened if he hadn't have been so dumb. Derek kicked at the ground. Of course, none of this would have happened if his mother had been on time either. Why did she have to be late? He leaned over and picked up a rock off the ground. Derek threw the stone out in front of him as hard as he could. It surprised him how good it felt, and so, as he continued to walk, every time he felt the urge to cry, he picked up a stone and launched it at the sky.

When he was within a mile from his house, Derek found a particularly big rock. He wound his arm way back and threw it with such force that it bounced twice off the ground. Derek noticed a fluttering movement in some high grass next to where it landed. Curious about the movement, Derek jogged over. The spot where he had seen the grass move was about ten or fifteen feet in from the road, and as he approached, the grass moved again. Derek tentatively reached forward and parted the grass with his hands.

Sitting there in the grass was a little bird; it was black and about the size of a small grapefruit. The bird had a sharp yellow beak and sequin-like eyes that reminded him of the eyes of a fish. Although it was small, whatever kind of bird it was, it appeared to be full-grown. The bird flapped its wings wildly and Derek could tell from the way it was moving that one of its wings was broken. Leaning over, Derek grabbed a long stick from the ground and used it to poke at the bird. It flapped around helplessly in a circle. Derek felt a tremendous sense of power; he was the only thing standing between this bird and its almost certain death. He thought about taking it home with him. If he could just get it to jump up onto the stick, he could smuggle it home under his shirt and nurse it back to health in his room. His mother would never know. He could hide the bird outside when he was at school and at night, he could keep the bird in his closet. It could be his secret pet! But as the bird continuously avoided latching onto the stick, like Derek had envisioned and hoped, his frustration turned into something much darker. Each time the bird dodged the stick, he found himself poking at it harder, until the animal cried out in pain. The sound of the bird's cries should have stopped Derek, but the crying only intensified his feelings of frustration and anger. Derek fell to his knees in front of the bird, jabbing at it merci- lessly with the stick. Only when the bird stopped moving did Derek finally lean over and pick up a large rock on the ground. Lifting it high over his head, Derek brought the stone crashing down onto the bird's skull. The bird did not move or put up a fight when he did—it was already dead.

Derek leaned back on his heels, panting, as he stared at the bird's tiny, black, lifeless body. The rock he had used to crush its skull fell from his hand and rolled onto the ground next to him. He wasn't exactly sure about what he had done. He felt the greatest amount of shame he'd ever felt, but that's not what made him cry. He started blubbering, great big childish sobs, not because he felt bad, but because some part of all of it had felt *good*—even wonderful. He leapt to his feet and ran the rest of the way home. He was still crying when he got there. His mother smiled as he raced straight from the front door to the shower, claiming his tears and shame for her own.

Angela had that same smug smile on her face now as she sat at the table with Derek in the crawl space. "Never made us late again, did you son?"

Derek pushed his food away and cast his eyes toward the wall. "I wouldn't have done that," he spoke up now, his voice was low and husky. "I wouldn't have done that if you had just been there."

"Well, you took care of that now, didn't you?" An evil grin spread across Angela's face as her image slowly faded from the table.

Chapter 6

Not long after the couples finished their meal above him, Derek heard the door to the back deck open and footsteps pad softly down the deck stairs. There was a rustling of bags and bottles under the deck. Derek quietly lifted himself up to peek out of one of the air vents to watch. Through the wire mesh he saw Lauren strategically lift and move around bags in the garbage can.

"Lauren? What are you doing?"

Both Derek and Lauren looked up towards the sound of Jason's voice. She quickly shut the lid to the trash can and peered up at Jason from the bottom of the stairs. "Nothing…"

"Don't give me that. Seriously, I hope you're not doing what I think you're doing."

"Can't I even walk outside without you following me?"

"No, because I know you," Jason said, walking down to meet her. "What did you throw out?"

Lauren crossed her arms and blocked the trash can.

"You gonna tell me?" He pressed. "You know I'm gonna look."

Upstairs, a now happily drunk Jessie stumbled outside to them, holding a glass of red wine. "What? Is the party moving out here now?" Her speech was slow and clumsy.

Matt joined his wife on the deck.

"Hey, does Jess have any weird habits?" Jason called up to his friend.

"I think it would be more notable if she had any *normal* habits."

Jessie gave her husband a light punch in the shoulder and giggled as she lost her balance.

"Whatever Lauren's doing, I'm sure there's a good explanation," Jessie said, lifting her wine glass in a toast.

"Thanks, girlfriend!" Lauren replied, dusting her hands off on her jeans, then moving up the stairs. Jason remained by the garbage can. "Just tell me it's not the leftover burgers."

"It's not the burgers," Lauren called back over her shoulder.

"Why doesn't that make me feel better?" Jason lifted the lid to the trash can and a guilty Lauren grabbed her friend's glass of wine at the top of the steps. Lauren took a quick swig and then quietly scooted back inside.

"What the? No, no, no," Jason said, shaking his head. "Not the burgers! These aren't even old!"

Jessie and Matt looked inquisitively over the railing as

Jason lifted out a rolled up paper bag with grease marks on it.

"Ohhhh," Jessie breathed, understanding now.

"What?"

"Leftovers," she answered her husband, as if that was enough of an explanation, and then went inside to join her friend.

"Leftovers?" Matt called down to Jason.

"Yeah," Jason sighed as he tossed the bag back in the bin and closed the lid. "Lauren's always had this weird thing about leftovers. I don't know why I have to suffer for it." He raised his voice, so that she could hear inside. "I was going to take those to work tomorrow!"

"You should be thanking me!" Lauren shouted through the open window. "They were on the counter for two hours! You'd die of salmonella if it wasn't for me."

"You can't even get salmonella from burgers, can you?"

Matt shrugged his shoulders at Jason, not knowing.

"Great!" Jason raised his voice again for Lauren's benefit. "I see some doughnuts are in there, too! Were *doughnuts* gonna give me salmonella?"

"They were right next to where you had raw bacon on the counter this morning!" Lauren called out from somewhere inside. When she reappeared in the open doorway holding her baby, Matt, who was still on the deck, looked taken aback. It wasn't that she was holding her baby that seemed to throw him, but rather *how* she was holding him; Landon was strapped into what looked like some sort of car-seat carrier.

"What if you had given him one of those doughnuts, huh?" Lauren asked, signaling to the baby. "What if he got some kind of food-borne illness? You would never forgive yourself." Lauren noticed Matt eyeing the carrier in her hand on the deck and stopped herself.

"Are we going somewhere?" Matt asked.

Lauren stared down at her baby, who was at ease in his car seat. Her eyes widened and she frantically searched out her husband as she realized what she was doing. When he saw what was happening, Jason dropped the lid to the trash. "Oh, the car seat? Soothes him! Little parenting trick!"

Relief washed over Lauren's face as her husband hopped back up the steps toward her. "Why don't you go put him down in the living room, babe? See if he nods off. If he doesn't, it's my turn tonight, right?"

She nodded, following his cue. "Right. Your night." She repeated.

"Yeah."

Lauren nodded politely to Matt and headed back inside with the baby looking slightly dazed. Jason turned back to Matt and smiled.

"Everything okay?" Matt's tone was kind, but his delivery suggested he hadn't completely bought their act.

"Yeah, we're okay." Jason cleared his throat.

The two men shuffled awkwardly for a beat, then Jason

turned his head toward the house and sniffed the air.

"You smell that?" Jason asked.

"What?"

"It smells like piss out here."

"Nah, I don't smell anything, man," Matt offered.

Jason sniffed the air again and followed the scent halfway down the deck steps. "Ugh, yeah, that's it. It smells like piss. Right here, on the side of the house. C'mere. Smell that?"

Matt walked over and smelled the spot near the side of the house. "Well, we know it's not your trash can," he said. "That thing's got fresher food in it than our fridge at home."

Jason shook his head then headed back up the steps to go inside. "Probably that stupid cat from next door again."

Matt followed his friend into the house. "That cat still bothering you?" Derek heard him ask just before they closed the door.

"They smell your piss-soaked, baby pants," Angela hissed in Derek's ear.

Derek ignored his mother as he looked sheepishly down at the cat loitering on the ground of the crawl space. Mr. Fluffy arched his back and rubbed his body up against Derek's legs. Derek picked the animal up and petted it in his arms. The cat purred and nuzzled against his chest, enjoying the long soft strokes. Derek felt guilty the animal was taking the blame for him; he'd be more careful where he went from now on.

Is this really the kind of stuff these people fight about?

Derek marveled to himself. *Cats in the yard and having too much food in the kitchen?* The Scotts were exactly like one of those sitcom families on television that had so fascinated him as a child—complete with canned laughter and sympathetic aws and oohs during the warmer "life lesson" moments. To Derek, they were perfect. Derek's mother was not as impressed, however. In his peripheral vision, he could see her pacing back and forth in the dark.

"I don't like this," she said. "I don't like these people at all—not one bit."

Later that night, long after their guests had gone, and Lauren, Jason, and Landon were fast asleep, Derek sat under the house thinking. He stared up into the darkness that was the ceiling of the crawl space, the floor of the Scotts' home. Not even a sky full of stars could have provided him a better glimpse of Heaven. He remembered Ms. Wendy's words to him in school: "Some people have an easier ride, Derek. That's just the way it is. But we are all born with the exact same clean slate and opportunities in life. Always remember that. You hear me, right? You understand? Nobody's born better. We can all have the exact same things. Some of us just have to take a couple of extra steps to get there is all."

Derek held the broken locks to the Scotts' kitchen window firmly in his hand, thinking how proud his favorite teacher would be of the steps he was taking now. He was taking control of his own life, his own…

"…destiny," Ms. Wendy finished the sentence for him in her signature, thick, Southern drawl.

This time, though, it sounded as if her voice was coming from right beside him instead of just in his head. "That's what it is. When you get on your right path, you'll know," she continued. Her sweet, young voice circled him. "Think of life like a river. When you find out what it is you're supposed to be doin' everything'll feel easy—like you're floating downstream. If you're on the wrong path, no matter what you do, it will always feel like you're paddlin' upstream."

Derek nodded at her words. His destiny. It couldn't have been any more obvious. All of the signs were there. The universe was bringing everything to him, carrying him down the river just like Ms. Wendy said it would: the shelter from the rain, the keys to the house (well, window latches), the endless supply of food. *This is my destiny.* Derek got to his feet and walked over to the door of the crawl space. The only problem, he thought as he pushed the door open, would be finding a way to get the Scotts to accept that *he* was part of *their* destiny as well.

The fluffy, white cat was now tired of the crawl space. Derek blocked the cat with his foot and narrowed his eyes at the animal as it tried to follow him out. The cat retreated backward as if sensing Derek's feelings. Derek wedged the door shut behind him and quietly climbed the steps to the back of the Scotts' home. He tiptoed from window to window. All of the windows were open, the cool night breeze drifting into the house through their flimsy screens. Derek couldn't see into the house, however, thanks to thick white plantation blinds that were all twisted closed.

Derek stopped in front of the big window to the left of the back door. It was the window to the main living area, Derek recalled. From where he stood right now, he would be facing the brown leather sofa inside. If he could walk through the wall, it would only take him about ten steps to be able to sit down on it.

Was that Landon crying?

The sound was faint, but as Derek brought his ear closer to the window he was sure of it. Deep inside the house and a little further to his left, he heard soft cries emanating from what must have been Landon's bedroom where Landon was signaling the need for food or comfort. Derek brought his hand up next to his face and rolled his head side-to-side against the top of the window as he listened.

We are all born the same.

He imagined himself sitting on the sofa in the living room, laughing and eating. In his mind's eye, he saw Jason next to him, ruffling his hair and jokingly putting an arm around his shoulder while Lauren brought them all glasses of iced tea. As Landon's cries grew louder, a light flicked on inside and the window to Derek's far right was illuminated. Through the open window he could hear the sound of Lauren's voice as she woke Jason up. "Babe? Baby's crying."

Jason groaned in response.

"Come on," she pushed. "You know I need you to come with me."

Derek heard some more tired groans—though from whom he couldn't tell—and could even make out the couple's footsteps shuffling across the hardwood floors, directly on the other side of the window from him. Seconds later, right in front of him, a light came on in the living room. Surprised, Derek took a step back from the window.

The baby's cries moved closer to where Derek stood and he ducked instinctively. When he did, he happened to notice one of the plantation blinds was flipped up at the bottom of the window, allowing him to see the Scott family through a thin slot. He watched as Jason walked into the living room, wearing nothing but some light grey boxer briefs and carrying his wailing son. Lauren, wearing a dark blue robe that looked practically lived in, was already seated on the sofa in front of them. Without ever looking back over her shoulder, Lauren held up a bottle for Jason to grab as he moved to seat himself and Landon past her; the perfunctory movement smacked of routine. While Jason sat down to feed the baby next to her, Lauren grabbed a breast pump that was seated on the cushion next to her and opened the top of her robe. Derek jerked his head up at the sight of her exposed breasts. *I shouldn't watch this. I'm too close*, he thought. He knew that if he stayed any longer, he risked being seen. He also risked losing everything he had worked so hard to get, and he had so much more left to do. He turned to go but made it only as far as the top of the stairs when something stopped him cold.

It was Lauren. She was singing. It was the most beautiful melody he had ever heard. The tune was unfamiliar to Derek. He listened as she sang something about babies and going to sleep, but the words didn't matter to him. The tone of Lauren's voice was unlike anything he had ever heard before. He could actually feel Lauren's emotions inside of each and every muted note carried over to him in the cold night air. She was in love. She loved her baby. But she was sad. She was frustrated. She was scared. She was…lonely. The hair rose on the back of Derek's neck. Derek wanted to go. He knew he needed to go, but he had lost all power over his body. It was as if she was one of those sirens who called sailors into perilous waters to their untimely deaths. Step by cautious step, Derek found himself helplessly drawn back to the living room window. When he reached it, Derek quietly took a seat on the deck and listened. With Lauren singing and Jason providing food and comfort, Landon's cries became softer and less frequent. Derek was mesmerized. *What would something like that feel like? To be rocked and comforted? We are all born the same.*

He refused to look through the opening in the blinds. He would give them their privacy. Anyway, it didn't really matter,

Derek could still perfectly picture Lauren and Jason on the other side, the baby wrapped in a warm blanket and cradled in his father's arms. His imagination was so good, he could almost feel the softness of the blanket and the warmth of Jason's bare chest himself. Derek's left eye twitched rapidly three times, a tick that had started a few years ago, but not another muscle in his body moved as Lauren repeated the song two more times. She then stopped singing the words and replaced the lyrics with "la la la's" and "da da da's." As Lauren did this, Derek heard another voice begin to hum over Lauren's.

"You can touch me if you want."

Derek swung his head around in the direction of the young girl's voice. It instantly transported him back to the first time he had heard it.

Derek was thirteen when he first met Erika. She lived in the large trailer park community he had to pass by on his walk home from school every day. Erika was fourteen. She was overly developed for her age and knew it. School was about to let out for the summer and she was sitting in a plastic lounge chair wearing a little, blue-denim bikini trying to take advantage of not only the sun but also an audience for her new found frame. She was wearing ear buds and humming along loudly to whatever song she was listening to. Derek pretended not to notice her, but Erika's eyes were tracking him beneath her dark, square sunglasses as he passed.

Dipping her sunglasses down with one finger, Erika called out, "Hey! Hey you!"

Derek turned around to see her propping herself up on her elbows, grinning seductively.

"Yeah, you. What's a matter? Don't ya like girls?"

Derek's cheeks turned red. He rubbed at the back of his neck, not knowing how to respond. Erika liked how she was able to make boys act like that now. She swung her legs confidently over the side of her chair and stretched her arms over her head. Her long, dirty blonde hair cascaded down and around her newly formed breasts as she did.

"You live in that trailer behind the park, don't ya? Must be nice to have so much privacy." Erika brought her arms down and waited for Derek to respond. "Well, what's your name?" she giggled, taking out her ear buds.

"Derek."

"He talks!"

Derek *did* like girls. He'd just never had a girl talk to him like this before. Erika could tell he was struggling, so she nudged him along.

"My mom's working, so I skipped school." Erika stood up as she said this and started walking toward the front door to the trailer behind her. "I have a joint. Wanna smoke it?"

Derek shrugged again and rocked back and forth on his feet.

"Well, I'm not gonna bite ya." Erika stopped at the entrance to the mobile home and posed with one arm on the door frame. "Unless you want me to, that is."

The baby had stopped crying inside the Scotts' home, but Lauren continued to hum from the other side of the window. Derek could barely hear her over Erika's voice now.

"You can touch me if you want to."

Derek remembered Erika reaching her arms back to undo her bikini top as she'd said this to him. He reached out now and gently touched the screen to the living room window as he had once touched her. His hand filled with pure wonderment.

"I mean, we can do whatever you wanna do. I see how you're looking at me."

Erika's trailer was filled with smoke. The two teens sat cross-legged facing one other, their knees touching. Erika's eyelids were heavy and her lips parted. A look of ecstasy crossed her face as she waited for Derek to do whatever he wanted. His hand gently grazed the curve that formed the side of her body as he scooted closer. Derek marveled at the soft-ness of her skin. Erika groaned and leaned her head back to-wards the ceiling.

"Please," she begged.

Derek took in her face. It was absolutely beautiful. Not exactly sure of what to do, he brought his arms up and circled them around her neck. As he moved his face closer to hers, her hair brushed across his cheek. She smelled like sunshine. It was intoxicating. Derek buried his face in the smell and the sensation was thrilling. Erika had said herself that they could do whatever he wanted to do, and in that moment he knew exactly what that was—he hugged her. Derek began to rock back and forth, hugging her hard. As he did, he started to cry.

Erika's eyes snapped open. Her body stiffened. This wasn't what she had expected. But then she got it. And dammit if she didn't need this kind of touch every bit as much as he did. Erika tenderly kissed Derek's head and returned his embrace.

Returning to the present, Derek found himself still sitting on the deck outside of the Scotts' living room window as the light turned off inside. The baby's cries and Lauren's singing had stopped. He imagined Lauren's face hovering over the baby's crib whispering, "Good night, baby."

"Good night, Mom," Derek whispered back.

Chapter 7

An assortment of men's clothing flew out of the open front door of the trailer. "Don't want 'em, don't need 'em!" Angela called out after the shirts and pants as they landed in the dirt.

Derek's mother had just broken up with another one of her boyfriends—if they could even be called that. An obvious junkie, Derek had noticed the man lurking around the house for the past couple of weeks. He'd never even caught the man's name. Angela shut the front door and hurried into the kitchen to grab a scrub brush off the counter. "Come here, help me," she instructed as she handed the scrub brush to Derek. Derek stood in the center of the kitchen holding the scrubber as his mother grabbed a bucket from under the sink.

"This is my life." Angela raised her voice to be heard over the faucet as she filled the bucket with water and soap. "My life. My money. My home." She smiled over her shoulder at her son with pride. "I got a job now—a real job."

Derek stared blankly back at her. He'd never seen his mother filled with so much enthusiasm. Once she had filled the bucket about halfway with water, Angela tossed in a sponge from the sink, shut off the faucet and walked over to Derek who was still holding the scrub brush she had handed him.

"Well, come on," she said, pulling her son down to the kitchen floor with her to clean. "This floor ain't gonna clean itself." Angela spoke quickly as she scrubbed next to her son.

"Just think, I've been doing this for free my whole life. Now someone's gonna give me money for it. Can you believe that? Sure, it may not seem like much—cleaning houses—but they don't know what I'm planning."

"You gonna use that?" She pointed to Derek's brush when she noticed her son wasn't scrubbing. Derek slowly began moving the brush back and forth next to her.

"The way I see it, I'll work harder than anybody else they got there—and I'm legal," she continued. "I'll get promoted within a year at least. Then?" Angela took a second to wipe her brow. Derek noticed how heavily she was sweating as she did.

"Then...then I'm gonna start a cleaning company of my own!" Angela rocked back to look at Derek. She was obviously eager for a response to this electrifying declaration. Her eyes were wide—too wide. Derek glanced up at her nervously but continued to scrub. In a rare moment of drug-induced clarity, Angela, maybe for the first time ever, seemed to actually see her son.

"Hey," she said softly. "Stop. Stop scrubbin' for a second."

She reached out and put a hand over his. Derek flinched at her touch. Tears stung the corner of her eyes. "Nobody ever showed me how to do this, ya know?"

Derek looked up at her, his body tense.

"I'm really gonna try. I'm gonna make our lives better." Angela took her hand from Derek's and wiped under her eyes. "Does that sound like something you'd like?"

Derek smiled his practiced smile. "Sure, Mom. That sounds nice."

Angela nodded and sucked in her breath. "Okay, then. What are we waiting for? Let's get cleaning."

Angela got down on all fours next to her son and resumed scrubbing the floor. She knocked her elbow into Derek playfully as she did. "A nice clean start. It's never too late to have a clean start, right?"

The morning light filtering through the crawl space vents seemed different to Derek. *He* felt different—more present somehow. Derek used an old rag to happily scrub away at the floor of the crawl space as the sweet melody of Lauren's lullaby from the night before played on a continuous loop in his head. Upstairs, he heard the Scotts' preparing for their day as well.

"Landon's gonna be late, Jason!" Lauren shouted from

somewhere above Derek. Loud footsteps, which could only belong to Jason, walked toward the sound of her voice.

"It's daycare," he heard Jason's muffled voice contend. "It's not like he's late for an exam."

"Pre-school," Lauren corrected him. "You know I hate when you call it daycare. Brrr. It's freezing in here! I'm going to shut the windows."

"Leave them open. It'll feel great in here by the time we get back from work."

Ignoring Jason, Lauren began closing the windows which not only shut out the cold but also shut Derek out of their conversation. Derek panicked in the silence as he realized he couldn't make out what they were saying anymore. *School? Why was Landon going to school?!* Nights of sleeping on the cold ground had made his muscles stiff. They felt as though they were tearing from the bone as he struggled to get to his feet. Craning his head toward the top of the crawl space, Derek tuned into the footsteps as they picked up overhead again. He tried to follow them, but they seemed to be going in a million different directions.

"It's Monday, stupid," a voice called out from within the crawl space.

Derek paused for a moment and looked in the direction of the voice. His mother appeared in the corner of the crawl space under the kitchen. She stood in the shadows, hunched over, smoking a cigarette. Unable to interpret what she was trying to tell him, Derek shook his head and tried once again to follow the sounds overhead.

"It's Monday," Angela said again, flicking the ashes from her cigarette on the ground. "They're doing what all perfect, television families do on Mondays."

Derek didn't stop moving but glanced nervously in her direction as she said this. The distraction made him trip over his own feet. His mother snorted as he fell to one knee. Not missing a beat, Derek popped back up and resumed his pacing.

His mother sighed, dropped her cigarette, and stubbed it out with her bare foot. "They're going to work, dummy."

Work? Derek froze mid-pace. He tried to unriddle the word in his mind.

"Work," Derek said, aloud this time. The word felt heavy and foreign on his tongue.

"Monday...school...work." Derek struggled to focus his thoughts as he turned all of these terms over in his mouth. Responsibilities and schedules hadn't been part of his life for a couple of years. These concepts seemed so alien to him now. The idea that any of these things could still exist—that they were still present in the lives of others—was jarring.

"Oh, come on!" His mother groaned. She ambled over to Derek, a foul, rotting smell trailing behind her. Angela put her hand on his shoulder and Derek felt a chill go up his spine as she brought her lips close to his ear.

"Now you can do what you want to do," she whispered.

"If they're gone? If they're not here…"

"I can go inside," Derek whispered, his eyes widening as he finished her thought.

His mother cackled loudly and slapped her knee. Derek had always hated her laugh. It was loud but flat. Her laugh lacked any of the joy and playfulness that laughter was supposed to convey. In spite of this, Derek felt his body begin to quake with excitement. He dug his hands into his pockets and pulled out the white plastic hooks to the Scotts' dining room window. His fingers trembled as he held the latches out in front of him.

Although Derek could no longer hear the family with the windows closed, above him, inside the Scott home, Lauren was now pulling meticulously labeled bottles of breast milk out of the refrigerator. "Did you remember the bag?"

Jason shouted back to her over Landon's cries from the other side of the house. "What bag?"

"The…just…nevermind," Lauren answered, more to herself. She put the bottles from the fridge down on the kitchen counter behind her. Just then, the doorbell rang.

"What now?!" Lauren walked over to the entryway and peered out of the tall, skinny line of windows next to the front door before opening it.

"Tom?" Lauren said, opening the door to find her neighbor, Tom Arthur, smiling at her. He waved his hand self-consciously in greeting.

"Hello, Lauren."

Tom was a friendly, stout older man, with thinning grey hair and big round cheeks. He and his wife Linda had lived in the home next door to them for more than thirty years.

"Hi, Tom. Is everything okay?"

Jason popped his head out into the hallway at the sound of their voices. "Morning, Tom!"

Tom stayed on the doorstep. "Sorry to bother you both so early, but I was out walking and I always see you both leaving around this time. Mr. Fluffy didn't come home last night."

"Who?" Jason called out from the hallway.

"Our cat," Tom said raising his voice and leaning into the open door. "You know, he's white and, well, fluffy? He likes your yard an awful lot."

Jason sighed, "Yeahhhh, she sure does."

"He," Tom corrected.

"Of course! Sorry, Tom, don't think we've seen him," Lauren said. Lauren tried to be kind, but it could be hard to shake Tom loose once he got started. He was retired and chatty, having long forgotten the pressure of time and schedules.

"Okay, well, we're just a little worried. He's never stayed out all night before."

Jason again called out loudly from the other room, "Sure she's…he's fine!"

"I'm sure he is," Lauren tried to soften the obvious annoyance in her husband's voice. "If we see him, we'll be sure to let you and Linda know right away."

"Okay, well…"

"We promise," Lauren put her hand on the doorknob and tipped her head back in the direction of Jason and Landon. "We're kinda in a rush right now. Two adults and a baby and all…"

Tom's eyes twinkled, "Oh yeah, I remember those days," he chuckled.

Jason appeared behind his wife now, trying to help her. "Okay, we'll keep an eye out for Mr. Fluffy. You take care now!"

Jason began closing the door with his foot. He had Landon on his hip and lifted one of the baby's chubby, little arms to wave goodbye. As the door closed, Tom called out, "You guys make sure to lock up real good when ya leave. They still haven't caught that guy who killed his mom up the road."

"Yup, thanks," Jason said as the door closed. Lauren could tell he wasn't even listening,

Lauren, who *was* listening, immediately opened the door back up. "What's that you said?"

Tom smiled, delighted to have an audience. "Don't ya watch the news?"

Lauren motioned to the baby on her husband's hip. "A little busy for the news these days."

"Well, it's all anyone's talking about," Tom explained excitedly. "Some guy who lived with his mom over off King Street, behind that big trailer park there, just up and killed his own mother." Tom leaned in and added in a confidential whisper, "Stabbed her like forty times. Cops think he might still be in the area, too."

"Oh my god!" Lauren gasped. She looked to Jason who had just noticed that Landon had spit up on his freshly pressed, white dress shirt. Lauren's discomposure was not lost on Tom, however, who immediately began to back pedal.

"Oh, I'm sure you guys are okay," he balked. "This guy was a real degenerate. High school dropout, drugs. Probably long gone. Still, you can never be too safe, can ya?"

Jason sighed as he rubbed at the spit-up on his shirt. "Right, okay. Thanks so much, Tom. We'll let you know if we see your cat, but we really have to get going."

Tom looked at his feet a bit embarrassed. "Sure. Sure. You young things get going." Tom turned to go and chuckled as he shot his hand up to wave goodbye. "Enjoy those nine-to-fives! Sure don't miss those!"

Jason closed the door, looking fully prepared for what came next.

"Oh my god, Jason!"

"This is why we don't watch the news," Jason grumbled as he walked into the hallway bathroom with Landon still on his hip. "There's something like this on every day, Lauren. It doesn't affect us. This guy has nothing to do with us."

Lauren followed her husband into the bathroom and stood watching him in the mirror as he dabbed water onto his shirt with his fingers. "Jason..."

"I don't have time for this right now, babe. I have my review this morning. I can't be late, okay?" Shifting the baby a little further out on his side, Jason grabbed a white hand towel off a hook hanging next to the sink and blotted his shirt. "I think we'd know if there was anything to be worried about. It's just one random guy."

"I'm gonna make some calls on the way to work and get someone out here to fix that window. I probably can't get anyone today, but hopefully someone can come tomorrow or maybe Thursday? I can go in late to work Thursday."

"One day, a few days, whatever. It's not going to kill us, Lauren. Jesus. Listen to yourself, you sound..." Jason stopped himself. "Sorry, I didn't mean..."

Lauren knew exactly what he'd stopped himself from saying. Her reflection in the mirror behind him hardened. "No, I get it." Lauren bit the inside of her cheek. "You're right."

Out of earshot below the Scotts, Derek was channeling his nervous energy into cleaning. There were so many layers of dust and grime on his "furniture" that it was going to take more than a little elbow grease to get it all off, but Derek was determined to make everything shine. He hadn't been able to hear anything that had been said above him since Lauren closed the windows earlier. He was, however, perfectly able to make out the squeal of the garage door opening when Lauren, Jason, and baby Landon all left for the day. Derek threw the cleaning rag over his shoulder and called out, "bye guys!" as it closed.

A couple of squirrels cheerfully chattered away somewhere in the trees above him as Derek pushed open the door to the crawl space. The white cat, just as eager as Derek to feel the fresh air, tried to follow him out, but Derek nudged the animal back inside with his foot before closing the door. "No, you don't. I'll get you something to drink. You just be patient."

Once he was sure the cat couldn't get out, Derek unconsciously began to whistle a sunny little tune as he hopped up the stairs to the back deck. Derek's mother watched him from down in the yard.

"Always too eager," she grumbled. "That's how you get caught."

Derek swatted at the air behind him for her to be quiet as he stood before the broken window. He leaned his body to the right at the top of the stairs and used both hands to first push up the screen and then the broken window that lead to the dining area and kitchen. Derek felt his breath catch at the ease with which they both opened. To make sure no one was watching, he glanced briefly to his left and right and then hoisted himself clumsily through the opening.

"You're going to get caught!" Angela chided from outside in a singsongy voice. "A dummy like you always does!"

Now inside, Derek used the dining table for support to stand up straight. He dutifully turned around and closed the window behind him, shutting out the sound of his mother's shrill voice. Turning back to face the kitchen, Derek smiled and inhaled deeply. It smelled so good in the house—so clean, like fresh-cut flowers and fabric softener. Suddenly embarrassed by his own appearance, Derek looked down at his fingernails. They were ragged and torn and there was black dirt packed deep beneath the nail beds. He shook his head. *Jason and Lauren certainly won't approve of this!* Shrugging his shoulders playfully, Derek moved confidently through the living room and into the hallway beyond it. There were three white doors in the hallway, two of them closed.

The only door that was open led to a large bathroom. *Perfect!* The house seemed to know his every thought! He walked purposely across the wide, white marble tiles and opened the linen closet across from the toilet at the far end of the bathroom. Derek whistled as he pulled out a plush, cream colored towel from the shelf. He laid the towel down on the dark granite sink counter. *This is going to feel good!* Derek chuckled to himself as he struggled to figure out how to work the shower handle. Once the water ran warm, he discarded his clothes on to the floor. He needed some clean clothes. Derek wondered if Jason's pants would fit him as he stepped inside the shower. The warm water felt deliriously good on his skin. He turned around in a big, slow circle, taking notice of the maybe half a dozen or so bottles of shampoo and soap lined up in the shower around him. Derek took the time to open each, deeply inhaling each new aroma. When he was done, he stepped out of the shower and wrapped the soft, cream colored towel he had placed on the sink around his waist.

There was a hard, little black plastic comb on the sink counter. Derek picked it up and ran the comb as smoothly as he could manage from the front of his scalp to the back. It was tough at first, but with each pass the comb moved more and more easily through his tangled, chin-length hair. As Derek watched himself in the mirror, the transformation was surprising. With the dirt gone and his hair brushed back, he looked like a wide-eyed kid again. He could pass for a real kid living in the Scotts' neighborhood. He could pass for Lauren and Jason's own child.

Derek opened the medicine cabinet. He sprayed perfume and colognes on himself. Next, he inspected everything in and around the sink's vanity. Sticking straight up out of a round, brushed nickel toothbrush holder, a bright yellow toothbrush caught his eye. Derek picked up the toothbrush and rubbed the bristles gently across his lips. He felt a charge of electricity at the dampness of the toothbrush; it must have just been used that morning by someone in the family.

Opening his mouth, Derek slowly worked the toothbrush around his teeth and gums, reveling in the intimacy of the act. It was like kissing someone. Not that he had that much experience—only Erika. Derek pulled the toothbrush out of his mouth and looked at it. He didn't want to think about Erika—not now. He rinsed the toothbrush off in the sink, placed it carefully back where he had found it, and picked his dirty clothes up off the ground.

With the towel still wrapped snugly around his waist, Derek wandered into the living room and stopped when he reached the fireplace. His eyes grazed over the amber colored egg that Lauren held so dear with complete disinterest. What did catch his eye, however, was a family photograph that sat on a little side table to the right of the fireplace. Derek shifted his dirty clothes under one arm and picked the photo up. He ran his hand over the smooth glass frame. The black and white image was a close-up of all three of the Scotts. Landon couldn't have been more than just a few weeks old in the photo. Although Lauren and Jason were both smiling into the camera lens, Lauren's smile seemed somewhat forced and unnatural. There was hesitation in Derek's hand as he gently returned the photo back onto the side table.

Continuing on, Derek toured the rest of the home, room by room, with great attention to detail. He spent hours touching fabrics, opening drawers, and inspecting knick-knacks. He committed every detail of the home to memory.

Derek even found a little pink shopping bag to stuff away the items he wanted to keep—items he assumed the Scotts wouldn't notice were missing. One of his favorite items, a lipstick, came from the Scotts' bathroom. There were maybe ten tubes of lipstick in the skinny top drawer of their bathroom vanity. Derek had opened every tube, smelled each one and then replaced the makeup exactly as he had found it. The only shade he chose to keep was the deep-red shade. It smelled like roses and crayons.

Derek couldn't believe the couple had a bathroom in their bedroom. Their bedroom alone must have been the same size as his entire trailer home. The walk-in closet in the Scotts' bedroom proved to be equally as impressive. Derek shook his head and laughed as he turned on the light and stepped inside. *The closet has its own light!* Derek could tell the left, significantly smaller side of the closet belonged to Jason. He reached into the seven or so different-sized, wooden cubby holes looking for something appropriate. It was almost comical as he tried on a pair of Jason's jeans; they fell completely off his wasted frame. Derek sighed, put on his old, torn jeans and folded Jason's back the way he had found them. *I can use the washing machine tomorrow to freshen up my own jeans*, he thought. Wanting to take something Jason wouldn't notice, Derek settled on a plain white T-shirt, which he plucked from a neatly stacked pile of at least twenty identical shirts.

Moving into the kitchen, Derek rearranged some spices on a shelf above the stove, so that they were all in sizeable order, and grabbed a cereal bowl out of one of the kitchen cabinets. He placed the bowl on the counter and opened the refrigerator to get some milk for the white, fluffy cat. A two-gallon jug of milk sat right in the center of the neatly organized refrigerator shelves. Derek removed the cap and drank straight from the container. The milk ran thick and cold against the back of his throat. He used his hand to wipe his mouth and then poured a small amount into the bowl behind him for the cat. Replacing the milk, Derek inspected the other items in the fridge. He paused as his eyes came to rest on four, crisp, bright red apples stored on the bottom shelf.

A couple of weeks after meeting Erika, thirteen-year-old Derek was lost in a daydream about her while he sat in his seventh-grade math class. A bell rang out, signaling the end of class, lifting him out of his fantasy. He felt a tug at the side of his face. Derek absent-mindedly reached his hand up to touch his eye, which twitched a few times in rapid succession. He took his time getting to his feet, lagging behind the rest of the other students. As he made his way to the door, his teacher, Ms. Wendy, called out for him to stop from behind her desk. "Mr. Fisher, would you mind staying behind a minute?"

Ms. Wendy was a petite and attractive young teacher whose Southern accent was about as subtle as her fire engine red lipstick. She had shoulder-length, deep brown hair and a heart-shaped face that almost always exuded a natural warmth and friendliness. However, today, as Derek looked back at her from the doorway, he thought she looked nervous.

"It's about your test," she said. Ms. Wendy cleared her throat as she scooted her chair back from her desk.

Derek walked toward her with trepidation. He hadn't been able to concentrate that well over the last couple of months. Things had been getting…jumbled. Ms. Wendy seemed to be able to register the concern in Derek's expression. She smiled in a way that lit up her entire face. "Oh no, it's fine. You're not in trouble or anything. You got the extra credit!"

Derek shrugged, not quite knowing what to do with the information.

"Well, don't let it get to your head too much," Ms. Wendy said, poking fun at his lack of reaction. "That's pretty impressive for a seventh grader, you know. I teach a calculus class over at the high school and most of my seniors would have trouble with that problem. Where'd you learn to do that?"

Derek shrugged again, this time embarrassed.

"Don't worry, I won't tell anyone and ruin your rep," Ms. Wendy winked. "I liked math a lot when I was your age, too. I realize it's not the coolest interest when you're a teenager."

Derek smiled a little. He liked the way Ms. Wendy talked to him. Lifting his hand in a self-conscious wave, he turned to go.

"Wait, before you go…" The nervousness Derek had heard before found its way back into Ms. Wendy's voice. "I… uh…while you're here, I have something you might be able to help me with."

Ms. Wendy used her hands to smooth out the skirt of her navy blue dress as she stood up. Her steps were so small and close together, she looked to Derek as if she were doing a little dance as she made her way over to the bookshelf near her desk. Derek watched curiously as she pulled a brown paper sack off one of the shelves.

"It's just a turkey sandwich and an apple, nothing too exciting. My husband packs it for me every dang morning. He's so sweet about it. I just don't have the heart to tell him I don't much care for turkey. I like to go out for lunch."

Her speech quickened with nerves as she brought the bag over to Derek. "I thought maybe, since I'm keeping your math secret, you could maybe help me with my secret? I could just leave it on the shelf here for you every day. You could take it, or throw it out or whatever…"

Derek's eyes narrowed. His mother had become increasingly forgetful when it came to buying food. Did Ms. Wendy know this? Had she been spying on him at lunch? He wanted the food, but he didn't like the idea of charity or of anyone feeling sorry for him.

"Why are you asking me?" Derek was surprised to hear the words come out of his own mouth. Questioning adults was not something he normally did.

Ms. Wendy's gaze turned more serious at the defensive tone in Derek's voice. She lifted the bag out toward him. "Because…I think we have a lot more in common than just math,

Derek."

He didn't know what Ms. Wendy meant by that, but something in the way she said it forced Derek's hand. As he reached out and took the lunch bag, Ms. Wendy's eyes softened.

"You know, if you ever want to learn some new math tricks or just hang out and talk, I'm here for about an hour or two after school every day. I'd love the company."

Derek opened the brown paper sack and pulled out the apple. "You keep this. Teachers like apples."

For a moment Ms. Wendy looked as if she might cry. "Thank you, Derek. That's very sweet of you," she said. Derek nodded, then awkwardly turned and headed out of the classroom, leaving Ms. Wendy holding the apple by her side.

Plucking a crisp, cold, red apple from the Scotts' refrigerator, Derek took a bite, smiled at the memory, and closed the door.

Chapter 8

Monday night, Jason arrived home a little later than normal. As he came through the front door, Lauren called out, "I'm in here!" from where she was preparing dinner in the kitchen.

"Man, traffic was a mess. Guess what came?" Jason asked as he struggled into the kitchen with a large package under one arm and Landon in his carrier in the other.

"Landon's costume?"

"Yup! Hey, can you help?"

Lauren quickly wiped her hands on a dish towel and then grabbed the package from under Jason's arm. Jason's disappointment with which item she had chosen to help him with briefly flashed across his face.

"The box was right on the front step. How did you not see it?" Jason asked her as he brought Landon over to the dining table to his highchair. Lauren placed the package down on the kitchen island then stepped over to the stove to peek into one of her pans. "I came in through the garage."

"But you didn't see it on the front step when you were pulling up?"

"If you haven't noticed, I have a lot going on." Lauren grabbed a box of puffed cereal off the counter as if to empha-size her point, and brought it over to the table for Landon to snack on. She poured about half a cup of the cereal directly onto the tray attached to his high chair.

"Did you move my spices around?" Lauren asked.

"Does that sound like *anything* I would do?"

"So weird. How was the review?"

"Still employed!"

"Well, that's a relief," Lauren joked as she left the dining table to get back to the package that she had left on the kitchen island. She grabbed a knife from the block next to the stove and began cutting along the seam of the packaging tape to open it. "Hey, don't eat my apples, okay?"

"Okay…"

Lauren lifted the knife in her hand toward her husband. "I mean it, I only bought five. They're supposed to be my work snack this week."

Jason chuckled, unaware of the missing apple Lauren was referencing. "Only you would count your produce."

She gave him a sideways smirk as she finished cutting the tape. Jason moved behind his wife to inspect the contents of the box. As Lauren opened it, she let out a dramatic sigh. "Oh, thank god! Talk about the nick of time. Halloween's only two nights away."

"See, you need to trust me," Jason said as she lifted the tiny, sequined pirate costume out of the box. "Kinda takes away from the fun, though—Halloween being on a Wednesday this year?"

"What? You and Landon planning an all-night rager?"

"Funny." Jason grabbed Lauren around the waist and spun her around to face him. "*You* better stay up late with me *tonight*. You remember what today is, right?"

Lauren nodded her head toward the food on the stove behind her. "Why do you think I'm cooking all this?"

Jason craned his neck to see over her shoulder. "Ooooh, are those collards with bacon, I see?"

"Not only that, I made cheesecake, too. Okay, I bought it, but we have it."

"I can't believe it. Man, five years in and you still manage to shock the hell outta me sometimes."

Still locked in her husband's embrace, Lauren's voice softened. "Look, I know I've been a little…intense…lately. I just want you to know, I get it. I'm working on it. I'm gonna relax a bit and try to get back to how things used to be. I love you."

"I love you, too." Jason kissed Lauren's nose. "But when I said, 'I can't believe you did this', I meant, I can't believe you cooked all this and didn't burn anything."

Lauren slapped her husband on the shoulders with her

hands. "Oh, shut up."

Lauren tried to wriggle out of his embrace, but Jason pulled her back into a cheesy dance position. "Come here, you."

She remained comically limp as he twirled her around. "We were destined for one another. The good, the bad, the burnt cooking—it was all meant to be. And you know what? I wouldn't have it any other way."

"Good, 'cause this is what you've got." Lauren managed to escape the dance and return to the stove to stir her collard greens. "How 'bout you give Landon a bottle and a bath and then go set the table up outside?"

"Outside? Someone's feeling romantic."

"We'll see how romantic I feel after everything is done."

"That's enough incentive for me." Jason went over and scooped Landon out of his high chair. "I'll give little man a bath and dinner and then set the scene. Heck, I'll even put the laundry away."

Lauren eyeballed her husband from her position at the stove. "Okay, romance level is totally rising."

"Babe, you must not know who you're dealing with." Jason cradled Landon with one arm and put his other arm on his hip, sticking out his chest. "Super dad is here. There's no problem I can't solve!"

"You forgot the two," Ms. Wendy said as she looked over

Derek's shoulder, solving the math problem in her head.

Derek furrowed his brow and looked up at her from his desk.

"May I?" she asked. Derek handed her his pencil. Ms. Wendy leaned over him and used the little pink eraser to erase his work. "I used to make the same mistake all the time."

She wiped away the little scraps of dirty paper and eraser shavings with her hand, then blew on his paper to get rid of any excess bits. Derek inhaled deeply as she did. Her breath smelled of the little strawberry candies she kept in a glass jar on her desk.

"See...you just carry this over...like this...and...voilà!" Derek smiled at her. "Cool, right?"

Derek nodded in agreement. He'd taken Ms. Wendy up on her offer to hang out after school a few times now. She lit up whenever he walked in the room; she always had some kind of snack and worksheet waiting for him. It made Derek feel special. He didn't care about the math all that much, although he let her believe he did. Ms. Wendy straightened up as she took in Derek's smile. She glanced nervously at the clock in the classroom, then out into the empty hallway. When she was sure no one was around, Ms. Wendy grabbed a chair next to Derek and took a seat.

"You know why I liked math so much when I was your age?"

Derek cocked his head to the side but said nothing.

"Because it felt really good to be able to solve a problem by using just a pencil and a piece of paper." Ms. Wendy paused, thoughtfully. "Do you know what I mean?"

Derek wanted to connect with her, but found he couldn't. Still, he held her gaze keenly. There was now a sadness in her eyes that he'd never seen before.

"Look, anything we say here stays between you and me. No matter what it is, okay?"

Derek nodded, still fascinated by her eyes. He thought about his science class where they'd learned about the many different kinds of snowflakes that were in the world. Her eyes made him wonder if there were that many different kinds of emotions in the world, too. As she continued to talk, Derek imagined Ms. Wendy's eyes filling up with snow.

"I shouldn't tell you this, but I know some things about you, from your file. And, well, I want you to know that you can talk to me. I went through a lot of the same stuff as you are, I think."

The snow fell harder in Ms. Wendy's eyes. Derek watched it blow and swirl as she continued.

"My dad ran off when I was real young, too. We didn't have a lot of money. I felt pretty alone a lot of the time..." Ms. Wendy's voice cracked.

This brought Derek back. He examined her closely as she seemed to shake off a chill.

"You know what helped me, though?" Ms. Wendy

slapped her hand down on his desk, her overly cheery demeanor returning almost too quickly. "Destiny!"

Derek furrowed his brow and a light smile crossed his lips as she jumped to her feet.

"Some people have an easier ride, Derek. That's just the way it is. But we are all born with the exact same clean slate and opportunities in life," Ms. Wendy explained as she began to pace back and forth in front of his desk with renewed energy. "Always remember that. You hear me, right? You understand? Nobody's born better. We can all have the exact same things. Some of us just have to take a couple of extra steps to get there is all. We're all the same, though. And we're *all* here to do something great. We're all here to help one another; to change someone or somethin'. That's our destiny! We all have one. Nobody's left out."

Derek's smile widened. He had no idea what she was talking about, but he thought the way Ms. Wendy was moving and flailing her arms about was funny.

"My destiny was to be a teacher. One day you'll find *your* destiny. And you know what? When you find it, you'll know. Think of life like a river. When you find out what it is you're supposed to be doin' everything'll feel easy." Ms. Wendy moved her hand up and down in front of her like a wave. "Like you're floating downstream. The universe will bring what you need to you. But if you're on the wrong path, no matter what you do, it will always feel like you're paddlin' upstream."

She brought both of her hands together in front of her chest as she came to a standstill. "You really have a talent, Derek. It could take you big places. Places you probably don't even realize are possible for you."

Taking in his smile and wide eyes, Derek could tell Ms. Wendy felt as though, in that moment, she was fulfilling *her* ultimate destiny. She beamed at him. "I have a surprise for you."

Ms. Wendy held up a finger for him to wait a second, her eyes twinkling. Derek watched, amused, as she hurried over to her desk and grabbed a pamphlet out of the top drawer.

"It's kind of a camp for kids going through stuff." Ms. Wendy brought the brochure over to Derek and placed it in front of him on his desk. Her voice buzzed with naïve enthusiasm. "You get to climb, go down rapids, camp and be out on your own for a few weeks. You realize you can do anything when you're out there."

Derek half-heartedly thumbed through the pamphlet. The pages were filled with brightly colored pictures of kids laughing and smiling in the sunshine.

"I'm a counselor there and, well, I'd like to take you there with me this summer."

Derek looked up at her, bewildered. "Really?"

"Really." A sly smile crossed Ms. Wendy's face. "That's if you want to, of course."

He considered the idea for a moment. "I don't have any

money."

"You don't need it. It's all covered. Do you wanna do it?"

Derek looked back down at the brochure in his fingers. Without meaning to, he began to feel his head nodding up and down. Wendy clapped her hands together in delight.

"Great! This is great!" she squealed. "Well, what are you waiting for?"

Confused, Derek lifted his eyes to her.

"Get up! Go and tell your momma!" Ms. Wendy ran around and scooted his chair out from under his desk. "Y'all will need to sign some forms and stuff, but I'll take care of the rest!"

Feeling uncertain, Derek picked the pamphlet up off the desk as he stood up to leave.

"This is going to be so great!" Ms. Wendy chirped.

Derek felt his feet begin to move faster as he exited the school and faster still when he reached the outer limits of the trailer park near his home. His lips were curled up in a smile and he felt a fluttering in his stomach. It was a strange sensation, but he thought it felt good. By the time he passed Erika's trailer, he was jogging. He didn't even notice her standing in her doorway, where she had obviously been waiting for him.

"Hey!" Erika ran out after him as he zoomed past. "Hey! Derek, wait up!"

Derek slowed to a fast walk as he called back to her, "Sorry! I gotta get home!"

"No, it's cool! Whatever!" She caught up with him quickly, her bare feet not even registering the sharp gravel at the edge of the road. "I'll be home alone tomorrow if you wanna come over. Hang out? I won't, like, attack you again," she joked, somewhat self-consciously.

Derek raised his hand up as he kept moving. "Okay, I'll come over after school!"

"Cool, okay!" His acceptance of her offer was all she needed. Erika stopped following. She twirled a finger through her hair and spun around on one leg, smiling, before heading back inside.

Derek's legs carried him swiftly down the long, dirt road to his home. He was so focused on his current mission that he didn't notice the strange, black pickup truck in the yard. Derek only stopped when he got to the front door, leaning over for a brief second to catch his breath. As he straightened back up, the door to the trailer swung wide open, nearly hitting him in the face. A man he didn't recognize walked out. The man was sweaty and the top buttons of his wrinkled dress shirt were unbuttoned, revealing an equally damp white undershirt. The man looked at Derek with surprise, then quickly shifted his eyes to the ground as he hurried past him. The swirling waters inside of Derek turned darker as he watched the man climb into his truck and drive off. When he was sure the man was gone, Derek slowly stepped inside the trailer. The air inside was thick and stale smelling.

"Mom?"

Derek was still holding the camp brochure Ms. Wendy had given him in his hand. His grip on the pamphlet tightened as he moved through the living room, creating a crease right down the center of the smiling face of the boy pictured on the front cover. Nothing in the trailer was out of place, but an uneasy feeling began to build in him as he made his way to his mother's bedroom. Sliding open the pocket door to her room, he found her. Angela was passed out on the bed, wearing nothing but a bra and a jean skirt. A cigarette, still burning, remained tightly held between her fingers. Something shifted inside of Derek as he stared at his mother on the bed like that. With no one around to see it, it went completely undetected, but the small flame inside him that had always wavered no matter how strong the wind, finally blew out.

As he walked to his mother's side, Derek didn't give the needles, plastic bags, or money on the bed so much as a second thought. Careful not to disturb anything, he removed the cigarette from her hand and stubbed it out in an ashtray on the side table next to her bed. Beside the ashtray he gingerly placed the camp brochure Ms. Wendy had given him.

Derek's face held the same vacant expression now as he pinned the soft white cat down with one knee and removed his hands from its neck. It had gone quickly. He had made sure of that. Derek liked the cat. He had not wanted to hurt it, but what other choices did he have? He didn't have a lot of time. He needed to introduce himself to the Scotts in a way that would let them know he was on their side. They hated the animal; they'd both said it. Regardless of how *he* felt about it, killing the cat was the grandest way Derek could think to prove himself to the family.

Chapter 9

The sun was setting beautifully, but the Scotts didn't notice the deep reds and purples that streaked across the sky through the open dining room window behind them.

"Look how cute he is!" Lauren squealed in a loud whisper.

Landon had fallen asleep in his highchair while seated at the table during their anniversary dinner. Food covered his face. He was wearing a dark-brown onesie pajama meant to look like a bear. There were ears on the hood and big paws for the feet. With his little, fuzzy paws poking out from under the food tray, Landon looked like an adorable, over-stuffed cub. Lauren and Jason both had their phones out, feverishly snapping pictures of the moment.

"Oh, this is a good one," Jason said, holding his phone out for his wife to see.

"Oh yeah, that's a keeper."

Lauren lifted her phone again to take another picture

when there was a knock at the front door. "Who's that?"

Jason tipped his chair back in order to see through the thin windows that were by the front door. Discovering the identity of the unknown visitor, he groaned. "Looks like it's our favorite neighbor."

"Again?"

Jason stood up from the table. "Ah, it's mommy and daddy time anyway, I guess." Jason smiled tenderly down at his sleeping son. "He sure is perfect."

"Yeah," Lauren agreed. In that moment, she felt the "old her" coming back. It startled her how such a quiet moment could carry such power. Jason seemed to notice the shift, too.

"If I put him in his carrier first, do you maybe wanna try putting him in his crib while I get the door?" Jason asked.

Lauren looked taken aback at first, but then nodded with a bit of nervous excitement and Jason jumped on the moment. Without any hesitation, he gently scooped Landon out of his highchair and transferred him into a carrier seated at the table, careful not to wake him. Another knock came from the front door. Jason buckled Landon into his seat then stole another quick glance at Lauren just to be sure.

"Get it. I'm fine," Lauren assured him. "I'll meet you on the deck." She reached across the table and gave her baby's fluffy foot a gentle shake as if to prove her point.

"I'm proud of you," Jason said.

Lauren stood up from the table with confidence. She was

proud of herself as well. "Thank you."

As Jason walked to the door to attend to their impatient neighbor, Lauren ducked behind him with the carrier. Landon's little bear ears bounced all the way down the hallway as Lauren ferried him to his room. Lauren heard her husband take a long, deep breath before opening the front door.

"Hey *again*, Tom," Jason said.

"Hi! So sorry to bother you again, but Mr. Fluffy still hasn't come home yet."

"Still no sign, huh?"

"Nope. It's just not like him. We went away on vacation once and he got loose for one day or so, but we were gone for a week. Scared the heck out of our friend who was watching him. We went to Riviera Maya, in Mexico? You ever…"

"Tom, we'll absolutely let you know if we see your cat," Jason interrupted. "But we're having sort of an anniversary thing tonight."

Lauren listened to the two men talking as she placed the carrier in the crib and unbuckled her baby. She hesitated for a moment as she took Landon out of his seat, almost bringing Landon to her chest, but then changed her mind at the last second. Instead, she laid him down on the mattress and hastily grabbed the carrier out of the crib. The little lambs printed on his fitted bedsheet seemed to bounce and dance as she did, but Landon didn't react at all to the movement.

You big chicken! She thought to herself. *Scared of a*

sleeping baby and dancing sheep. Me and Jess used to climb the highest water tower in four counties, high as kites, with nothing to light our way but the moon! What happened to that girl? She reached down and lightly caressed the side of Landon's face with the back of her hand. His peace was so effortless. *We all start out that way.* Lauren marveled to herself. *Isn't it funny how much work it takes to get back to who we were in the first place?* Tom's incessant chatting down the hall pierced Lauren's inner monologue. She chuckled to herself, thankful for the distraction. *Man, that guy can't take a hint, can he?*

"When you're gone a long time like that, cats can get lonely or confused, you know? But we've been here the whole time." Tom repeated what he'd said before. "It just doesn't make sense."

"Uh-huh," Jason agreed. Lauren saw him lean his head wearily against the doorframe as she exited the baby's room. She gave Jason a "thumbs up" and then motioned to him from the hallway to shut the door where Tom couldn't see.

"You two ever been to Mexico? It's really a romantic place for…"

"Okay, Tom, the wife's waiting. I have to go," Jason said hastily, abruptly shutting the door on a still-talking Tom. "I'll be sure to let you know right away if we see him!" Jason yelled through the closed door.

"I can't believe you did that!" Lauren clapped her hands to her mouth to cover her laughter.

Jason sauntered into the kitchen, evidentially quite proud of himself. He lifted a bottle of wine and two glasses off of the kitchen island and nodded toward the back door. "Shall we?"

The sound of the couple's laughter traveling outside of the house and onto the deck excited Derek. He stood up, bringing the cat with him to the crawl space vent nearest to where the couple was. He hugged the dead animal close to his chest. Its body was still warm. As Derek pressed his ear to the vent to better hear Lauren and Jason, somewhere in the distance he could also hear an older man's voice, calling out, "Here kitty kitty! Here kitty kitty kittyyyy!"

"Ugh, poor Tom," Lauren groaned as she poured herself a healthy amount of wine. "For all the crap we say, I hope he finds him."

"I can't believe I'm saying this, but maybe I'll go help him look tomorrow." Jason grabbed the wine bottle from his wife and poured himself a glass.

"Whoa," Lauren joked. "Sure you should be drinking? You sound pretty drunk already. You're going to help Tom look for his cat? Is that what you said? The cat you hate?"

"Ahhh, their kids are grown. That damn thing is probably like their kid. One day, I might be that old man looking for his lost cat."

"Ya big old softie." Lauren punched Jason lightly on the arm. She lifted her wine glass and swirled the deep red liquid inside—cabernet, her favorite. Lauren took a thoughtful sip, before redirecting the conversation. "You know, I wanted to talk to you about the window in the kitchen.

"I knew this was coming."

"This has nothing to do with what Tom said this morning about that guy who killed his mom."

Jason raised an eyebrow skeptically. "Really?"

"Really." Lauren said this so matter-of-factly, she almost believed herself. "But it got me thinking. It's a safety risk. We have a kid now…"

"We already said we're fixing it."

"Yeah, I got an appointment for Thursday, but that's not…"

Jason interrupted his wife. "Thursday? You know what? While I'm thinking about it, when we do that, why don't we lock up the crawl space for the winter, too?" Jason peered down at the yard from his seat on the deck. "Grass is done growing for the year."

"Yeah, fine. Window fixed. Crawl space locked. Got it," Lauren said, trying desperately to get back to her point. "I was *thinking*…maybe we should get an alarm system, too. Something nice. Cameras, maybe?"

Jason set his wine glass down on the table. "Daycare's already killin' us, babe. You really want to spend money on some overpriced security system?"

"Funny how we had enough money for your new television and car, though."

"Hey, I didn't even want that car. You're the one that said we needed something bigger with the baby."

"Whatever. They probably don't even cost that much now. And can you really put a price on safety?"

"Yes. Yes, you absolutely can," Jason laughed and nodded toward their home. "It's not like this is some low-rent place. Bad things don't happen in neighborhoods like this. Besides, do you want to have money for a really nice family vacation somewhere or do you want to spend thousands of dollars on unnecessary cameras?"

Lauren cocked her head to the side, surprised. "A family vacation? Where were you thinking of going?"

"Nowhere for the next thirty years with all the money it's going to take to build that fancy addition onto the house."

"What fancy addition?"

"The panic room you're probably going to ask for next."

Lauren laughed and took another sip of wine. "Fine, point taken. Let's change the subject." She would never let her husband know it, but she secretly loved how he didn't put up with any of her crap. "Where are you taking us on this amazing family vacation?"

"Come here, you!"

Lauren's wine splashed up from her glass and onto her shirt as Jason grabbed the arm of her chair and scooted her close to him. She opened her mouth to complain when he kissed her. The kiss was stronger than Lauren had been expecting, and she felt a long-forgotten desire awaken within her.

In the darkness of the crawl space Derek's fingers dug into the fur of the dead cat he was holding. They were shutting him out? The idea caved in on him. He strained to hear more of their conversation through the crawl space vent but, for the next minute or so, the couple stopped talking. Derek could only make out some wet smacking sounds and intermittent light moans. Then there was a whisper from Lauren: "Unzip your pants."

"What? Out here?" Jason whispered back, surprised.

"It's getting dark, nobody can see."

There was some rustling followed by the sound of a zipper hastily being unzipped.

"What's gotten into you?"

"Shh. Stop talking."

Derek was furious. *How can they be acting like a couple of horny teenagers at a time like this? How can they do this to me after everything I've done?* He placed a hand down on the handle to the crawl space door. This was it. He was going to show them! But just as he was about to pull the door open, "Here kitty! Here kitty kitty kitty!" came booming from around the front of the house. Lauren popped her head up at the sound of Tom calling for his cat again.

"Ugh, okay, I can't listen to Tom and do this…"

"No. No. Keep your head there!" Jason protested.

"What?!"

"No! Not keep your head *there*. I mean, keep your head in the game! Stay in the moment...just...here." Jason grabbed the wine glasses and bottle from the table. His pants were hanging comically off of him as he waddled to the door. "We'll just move this inside."

One of the wine glasses slipped as Jason opened the door to the house. Jason caught the tumbling glass mid-air, nearly falling through the open doorway as he did. Lauren found the power she felt deliciously seductive. She moved slowly to him, not taking her eyes off of his. When Lauren reached the door, she grabbed the back of Jason's head and pulled his lips to her mouth. "Take me inside and do me hard."

Derek listened on, ruined, as the couple toppled through the open doorway. He could hear the sounds of their love making overhead as he began pacing the floor of the crawl space. Fixing the window was one thing, but locking the crawl space? *After everything I've done, they're going to lock me down here?* His mind raced. What had he done wrong to deserve this? What had he done wrong? As Derek thought hard about what exactly it was he had done wrong. Flashes—scenes from what seemed like somebody else's life—suddenly spliced themselves into his racing thoughts.

Blood. Fists. Hair. Derek saw Angela on the ground. He saw a pair of hands plunging a knife into her chest over and over again. Derek hit his head with his hand, trying to stop the images. What had he done?

Chapter 10

Erika's breath was hot against Derek's face as she broke their kiss to take another hit from her joint.

"It's laced with PCP," Erika somehow managed to say while still holding her breath.

Derek watched as she blew out a large cloud of smoke. They were sitting on the floor of her bedroom. The smoke hung between them like a ghost.

"They call it greens or something." Erika's eyes were glassy. She coughed as she handed him the joint. "I fished it outta my aunt's purse. She's gonna freak when she finds it missin'."

Derek inhaled the sweet tasting smoke deeply, thinking of nothing, as his eyes scanned Erika's room. It was small, about the same size as his. There was no real furniture, only a mattress with black sheets and fuzzy hot-pink pillows on the floor in the corner. On the walls were photographs, posters of bands Derek wasn't familiar with, and quotes and song lyrics that she had handwritten using an assortment of different colored markers.

"I know about your mom, ya know."

Derek watched Erika pluck the joint from between his fingers as she said this. He marveled over how he could see her touching him but couldn't feel her fingers. His head felt funny, like his brain wasn't in his head anymore, like it was somewhere else in the room. Erika held the smoke in her lungs again but let it go prematurely this time.

"Holy crap!" she exclaimed as she started coughing. "Do you feel that?"

"Why did you say you know about my mom?" Derek heard himself ask. "Know what?"

Erika sat back on her heels. "Just that she...ya know, does stuff for money sometimes." Erika picked at the stained tan carpet beneath her with one hand as the joint burned away in her other. "My aunt and uncle got in a nasty fight over her once."

"What? Did she do something for your uncle?" Again, Derek could feel himself speaking, but it was more as if he was watching the conversation unfold instead of being an active participant.

"It was dumb," Erika shrugged, now uncomfortable. She continued looking at the carpet, trying not to make eye contact. "He said, like, she gave him a handy for cigarettes or something."

Derek's eye twitched as he stared blankly ahead. His blank stare contradicted the profound, unrecognizable emotions that suddenly swelled deep within him. Erika sidled up next to Derek on the floor and leaned her head against his shoulder.

"You know, I had a shrink the state made me see for a while." Erika paused and lifted the joint to her lips. "She said... like...I dunno...some women get slutty if they've been abused and stuff...like...if someone's done something to 'em." Erika inhaled deeply and blew out the smoke. "Maybe that's what happened to your mom."

Erika held out the joint for Derek, but he didn't take it. He kept staring into the empty space ahead of him, expression-less. Erika looked hesitant and when she spoke again, her voice was softer.

"My...uh...my dad...did some stuff to me. Well, step-dad anyway. I was really little and I don't remember. That's why my mom left him. But, I dunno, maybe that's why I some-times come on a little strong?"

Erika looked at Derek. He guessed she was waiting for a response, but he remained silent. She seemed uncomfortable with his silence, like it made her nervous. Wiping a lock of hair out of her face, she shook her head, as if shaking out the mem-ory, and lifted the joint to her mouth. As she blew out the smoke, Derek began to chuckle to himself. Erika looked over at him, curiously amused. She giggled too, not knowing why, but wanting to join him. She stopped, however, as his laughter grew.

"What are we laughing at?" she asked.

Derek fell forward, laughing. "You fucked your dad!" he yelled, slapping his hands to his thighs. "You fucked your dad! You fucked your dad!"

Erika's face fell.

"You fucked your dad. You fucked your dad!" Derek didn't know why he kept screaming the same hurtful phrase over and over again. His body, now entirely out of his control, rolled on the ground as he roared with laughter.

"Shut up!" Erika slapped his body with her hands. "Shut up! I said, shut up!"

When her slapping failed to stop Derek's cackling, Erika jumped to her feet and kicked him. The scent of cheap, powdered, floral deodorizer filled his nose as his face smashed into the carpet. Erika struck Derek hard in the shoulder with the heel of her foot. She meant business. "Stop!" she cried out. The pain in her voice was low, raw and desperate.

Derek lifted his hands to protect his head. Still unable to catch his breath, he caught sight of Erika's face as he tried to roll himself up off the ground. Her tears fell with such force from her eyes they barely had time to touch her cheeks as they splashed onto Derek's body. "Why are you doing this?" she sobbed. "Why? Stop it!"

Erika grabbed Derek by the arm and tripped as she attempted to pull him up. "Get the hell outta here!"

Derek sucked his breath in hard, but another fit of laughter burst out of him. Erika yanked him by both arms now. Maybe she wasn't strong enough to pull him up, but she sure as hell could drag the bastard out! The water-stained ceiling above Derek began to move across his field of vision like a conveyor belt. He laughed the entire way as Erika dragged him across the floor to the front door. Once at the front door, Erika used her hands and feet to push Derek outside. "Don't you ever come back here!" she screamed. Derek rolled down the trailer's two front steps into the dirt. "I don't ever want to see your face again! Ever!"

Erika's breath caught on nearly every word. She held firm in the doorway—possibly waiting for one last word, an explanation maybe, anything that could help her make sense of the absolute horror of what had just happened with a boy she thought was her friend. Derek lumbered to his feet. He held his stomach, which hurt from laughing. He tried to talk—to tell her he didn't know what was happening, but his words only came out as more chuckles. It was as if his brain was a computer and someone had gone in and switched all the wires around. Erika glared down from the trailer at him with pure hatred. "You're a horrible person."

Chapter 11

Derek had walked up the back stairs to the Scotts' home a number of times now, but this time it was different—he wasn't hiding anymore. With Mr. Fluffy dead in one hand, Derek climbed the wooden steps deliberately. A cockroach scuttled out of his way as he reached the landing. Lauren and Jason had turned off the lights and gone to bed hours before. The home was completely dark as he entered without a sound through the dining room window. Knowing exactly where he was heading, Derek crossed the living room, travelled down the short hallway, and stopped once he reached the door to the baby's bedroom.

Landon's door was already slightly ajar and Derek used his foot to swing it the rest of the way open. A small stained glass night-light, made to look like stars in the sky, cast a blue glow across the floor and the fuzzy, white area rug positioned in the center of the room. There was a bookcase on one side of the nursery that was filled with picture books, as well as an array of plush stuffed toys. Next to the bookshelf sat a big, soft, beige recliner. On the other side of the room there was a dark wooden changing table and behind it a crib made of matching dark wood. From where he stood in the doorway, Derek could just make out the outline of Landon's small body sleeping in the crib.

Derek made his way over to the baby, quietly. When he reached him, he stared blankly down at him over the crib's protective side rails. Landon stirred momentarily, his eyelids fluttering like the wings of a butterfly. Derek felt a deep hatred stir inside of him. He hated how warm the baby was, how peaceful he was. He hated his lips that would always know kisses, his full belly that would always know food, and his small fingers that would always have a hand that wanted to hold them. Reaching down into the crib, Derek placed Mr. Fluffy against Landon's head. Landon stirred again and nuzzled his face into the soft, white fur of the animal. Derek watched the baby, expressionless, for a few more minutes before slowly exiting the room. *It was time*, he thought. Things hadn't gone the way he'd wanted with the cat, but he wasn't giving up. He had a plan this time. The Scotts were going to accept him, but he had to move fast. He needed to stop dilly-dallying, as his mom would say. It was time to get what he had come for.

Slipping into the bathroom next to Landon's room, Derek walked purposely toward the linen closet. He'd memorized the contents of nearly every shelf in it. Even in the dark, Derek was easily able to lift out exactly what he needed—a single white sheet, which he plucked from a neatly folded pile of bedding. With the sheet tucked under his arm, he then moved stealthily back through the hallway, the living room and out to the kitchen on the other side of the house.

He stopped at the edge of the kitchen, just outside of Lauren and Jason's bedroom, where a black butcher block of knives sat next to a stainless steel toaster on the granite countertop. From the block, Derek pulled out a single, medium-sized knife. Derek felt a swell of pride as he gripped the sturdy, black handle of the knife and held it by his side. He now had both of the items he needed from the house. The knife and the sheet were going to be his keys to salvation—he knew it. Derek also knew he should be going. He had what he had come for after all, but the door to Lauren and Jason's room that hung halfway open, only a few short steps away from him, proved too enticing. *Just one little peek,* he reasoned, and then he'd go.

The wooden floors creaked ever so slightly beneath his feet as he approached their room. Using the door to hide his body, Derek poked only his head into the opening. The lights were off in the couple's room, but the glow from a tiny night-light in their bathroom provided just enough light for Derek to be able to see. In the dim room, Derek could make out Jason and Lauren lying in their bed that was centered in the room. The foot of the bed was only a few steps away from where Derek stood behind the door. Jason was sleeping on his right side, facing the bathroom on the left of the room. Lauren, who was asleep on her stomach, had her head facing the bedroom window on the right side of the room.

Using the hand that held the knife to nudge the door open a bit more, Derek was startled to see his mother, Angela, staring at him from under the bed. Her flesh was rotting off of her and her eyes were sunken deep in her skull. A wide, grotesque grin spread across Angela's face as she stared at her son's shocked face. Derek opened his mouth to speak, but Angela held a decaying finger up to her lips for him to be quiet.

Trying his best to ignore his mother, Derek silently entered the room. He moved to Lauren's side of the bed and loomed over her, watching her breathe. Lauren's hair was loose and cascaded in big waves down and around her pretty face and onto her pillow. Derek reached his hand out to touch the silky tendrils, but just as his fingers made contact, Jason moved next to her. Derek snapped his hand back immediately and ducked down on Lauren's side of the bed to conceal himself. He heard Jason groan. Derek then watched the mattress next to him move from Jason's weight as he got out of the bed in the dark. Angela's corpse-like hand slithered out from under the bed, her withering fingers beckoned Derek to come join her. Derek did as he was told and slid under the bed next to his mother. Once under the bed, Derek caught a glimpse of Jason's socked feet moving across the carpet into the bathroom.

Angela held her boney finger to her lips again. She

smelled like rotting flesh. Derek breathed quietly through his mouth as he listened to the steady stream of urine coming from the bathroom. The toilet flushed. Derek felt himself grip the knife tighter in his hand as Jason's feet approached the bed. The mattress sank down under Jason's weight, pressing on top of Derek's body. Derek, very quietly, repositioned himself, rolling carefully from his side onto his back, where he was more comfortable.

Staring wide-eyed into the mattress above him, Derek heard Lauren's groggy voice speak to Jason. "C'mere you."

"What are you doing awake?" Jason asked, surprised.

"I can't stop thinking about earlier. That was so hot."

Derek's eyes widened as he heard what sounded like kissing. Then he heard Lauren whisper, "Ready for round two?"

The bed moved and shifted above Derek, eventually settling into a soft, rhythmic pounding. Derek slid his hand into his pants and moved with the same tempo, speeding up when they did and releasing when they did. But when Lauren and Jason fell back asleep, Derek remained alert. He stared into the mattress above him for hours. In fact, he had only just begun to nod off when he awoke to the sounds of Lauren's terrorized screams the next morning.

Chapter 12

"Lauren?! What's going on?!" Jason cried out as he leapt out of the bed. He ran as fast as his legs could carry him toward the sound of his wife's blood-curdling screams. He found Lauren in the baby's room, her face was flush with terror. She had Landon on the floor in the center of the room where she was frantically buckling him into his carrier seat. Landon, upset by the loud voices, began wailing as well.

"The crib!" Lauren managed to get out. "Look in the crib!"

Jason whirled around and stared down into the crib behind him. "What the hell…?"

Lauren shot out of the room with Landon firmly strapped into his carrier seat. And before Jason could even process the image of the dead cat in his son's crib, Lauren was already on her phone calling the authorities.

When the squad cars pulled up to the home, the Scotts were waiting anxiously in the driveway to lead them inside.

Alongside them stood their somewhat shell-shocked looking neighbors, Tom and Linda, whom Lauren had frantically dialed the moment she hung up with the 9-1-1 dispatcher. The two policemen, who had arrived to the panicked call of a break-in, shot sideways glances at one another behind Lauren's back, as she paced the length of the living room. The fact that Lauren was wearing a cartoon nightshirt over her jeans was not helping her efforts to get the police to take her more seriously.

Lauren threw an exasperated hand out toward Jason who was holding Landon on the sofa. "Should we go to a hotel? Are we safe here?"

A third cop walked out of Landon's room, carrying the dead cat in a trash bag. He brought the bag over to Tom and his wife who stood stoically by the front door. After an awkward hand off, the officer offered his condolences to the older couple and left through the front door.

"Should he be going?" Lauren asked incredulous as she watched the officer leave.

Mike, the taller of the two officers still in the living room, nodded to his partner to signal he was going to take the lead on this. "You said the cat comes...uh...*came* over here a lot, right?"

"Yes, officer. That's correct," Jason answered. He looked tired. Landon bounced happily on his knee, excited by all the people in the home.

"But the cat was in Landon's crib," Lauren interjected. "I

mean, someone would have had to put it there, right? How else would something like that happen? Do you think someone broke in here?"

The cop that was hanging back by the door rolled his eyes at his partner, Mike. Mike took Lauren by the arm. The effortlessness in the way in which he gently guided her over to the sofa to sit down spoke volumes about his experience in the field. There was enough room on the sofa for all of them, and after he seated Lauren next to her husband and baby, Mike sat down as well.

"Ma'am," Mike said with a sincere tone. "There's no evidence that anyone broke into your home. Do you have any reason to believe someone would?"

"Well, I mean..." Lauren glanced over her shoulder at her neighbors who were still standing in the doorway. "Tom told me about that man on the news who stabbed his mom. The guy you all are looking for?"

Jason let out a labored breath. "Oh, Lauren..."

Lauren didn't care for the audible annoyance in her husband's voice. "Well! What if he killed the cat?! Have you guys caught him yet?"

"It's okay, sir," Mike said, smiling warmly at Jason and then calmly readdressing Lauren. "Ma'am, you always want to look for the most logical explanation first. It's been nice out. Have you two had your doors or windows open?"

Lauren felt her face immediately begin to buzz with heat

and embarrassment. It appeared Jason was making the same connection she was.

"Oh, yeahhh," Jason groaned. "We were drinking wine outside last night. The door was open while we were..." Jason paused. Lauren could tell he was racking his brain for how best to dance around their drunken, semi-public, possibly illegal sexual exploit in the open doorway from the night before. "The door was open while we were...taking things back inside." Jason cleared his throat as he glanced at his wife. "It took a while."

Officer Mike smacked his lips together, making a popping sound. "See? Always a logical explanation. Cat probably got in then. Got scared and hid in the baby's room. Got stuck in the slats of the crib. Or even the baby could have..." Mike nodded at Landon who was happily gnawing on his father's shoulder. "Well, babies don't always know what they're squeezing..."

Tom's wife, Linda, choked back a sob from the doorway. Lauren glanced at her neighbors sheepishly. She had forgotten they were there. She nodded, trying to accept the logical explanation Mike had offered to her, but something nagged at her subconscious, making her press once more. "But the guy you're looking for? Did you catch him yet?"

"Lauren, enough," Jason said evenly.

"What? I'm asking..."

"Officer, you'll have to excuse my wife," Jason interrupted. "She's been battling postpartum depression. She's just now getting back to herself."

Lauren's eyes shot daggers at her husband.

"No, it's fine," Mike said to Jason. "Ma'am, you all don't need to worry about him. This is a kid we're looking for; high school dropout, drugs are involved. His mom was no stranger around the precinct."

Mike looked over his shoulder at his partner. "Remember Angela?" His partner smirked at the question, obviously recalling some professional interaction with the woman. "That woman was a piece of work. We had no idea she even had a kid." Mike sucked in his breath through clenched teeth as he shook off a chill. "Still, no matter how mean, nobody deserves to go like she did. Takes a special kind of monster to do what he did to her."

In the doorway, Tom's wife buried her head into her husband's shoulder to muffle a cry. The entire room went silent as everyone looked uncomfortably at Tom and Linda.

Mike stood up. "Anyway...when you've been in this business as long as we have, you see this all the time. Kid didn't have a chance. It's just a cycle. Pretty sad, really. He's probably hiding out with friends somewhere. Kids talk. We'll find him. You just lock up real good. Keep your lights on when you're away. Keep the bushes trimmed down nice in the front by the windows. This is a nice neighborhood. You'll be fine."

Lauren followed Mike to the front door where he stopped

to address Tom and Linda. "We're sorry 'bout your pet, folks."

"Yes," Jason said, getting up from the sofa with Landon to join everyone at the doorway. "Truly, we're so sorry."

"We really are," Lauren agreed. "If there's anything we can do…"

Teary-eyed, Tom nodded politely and hugged his wife. As the two policemen followed the heartbroken couple down the front steps, Jason called out, "Thank you, officers!"

He closed the door softly behind them and turned around to face Lauren who was waiting for him.

"You're an ass," Lauren said.

Jason brought Landon to his car seat carrier in the living room as Lauren stormed into the adjoining dining room. "You're overreacting, Lauren."

With intense anger, Lauren began shoving daycare items into Landon's diaper bag at the dining table. "Of course I am. I'm the crazy baby lady. I couldn't possibly have a thought or concern that was rational."

"Lo…."

"No. Don't 'Lo' me. You can drop the whole supportive husband act now."

"Right, 'cause this has been so easy on me. I didn't get months of paid leave for this. For the first few months, I was mom, dad, *and* had to work fifty hours a week. I couldn't even look in your direction without wondering if it was gonna set you off. Where was my support, huh? Excuse me if…"

"Yes, excuse you!" Lauren roared. "I'm sorry my mental break has been so inconvenient for you!"

The baby started to cry in Jason's arms. Jason brought Landon to his chest and snuggled him. The action was so instinctive and unintentional that it set off a series of explosions in Lauren's body. Each blast of shame, resentment, and anger that hit her felt so strong, she was sure they would knock her off her feet. Jason lowered his voice as he gently placed Landon into his carrier on the living room ground in front of him. "Like it or not, you *are* getting over postpartum depression."

Lauren lowered her voice, too, but the passion behind her words remained. "I don't have a problem with that. What I have a problem with is constantly being reminded of it. This is how everyone is going to see me for the rest of my life. This is going to define me, not because I won't get over it, but because the rest of the world won't get over it."

Adrenaline surged through her body like a drug. It deposited its signature aluminum-like taste on her tongue. It made her skin buzz. The seconds seemed like minutes as Lauren waited for Jason to say something back. But Jason said nothing at first. He didn't even look in her direction as he meticulously tightened the carrier's straps over his son's shoulders. It was when Jason clicked the seatbelt across Landon's lap that he finally broke. Jason dropped his head and choked back a sob. "How long's this going to last?"

"What?" Lauren was taken aback by the sudden display

of emotion coming from her husband. In all their years together she'd never once seen him cry.

Jason lifted a defeated hand out toward their baby in his carrier seat. "There was a dead animal in the crib with him, Lauren. If that doesn't make you want to comfort him, what will?"

Jason's words fell on Lauren with such crushing weight that she struggled to find the air she needed to breathe, let alone speak. "It's not that...I...don't want to. God, of course I *want* to. Is that what you think of me?" Big round tears streamed down her face. "I want it more than anything. I love him so much. I'm scared. What if I...? What if...I'm scared of *me!*" Lauren crumbled to the floor with her admission, her shoulders heaving with great big sobs.

"Oh, Jesus," Jason said, running to where his wife was and leaving Landon safely buckled in his carrier seat in the living room. He fell to his knees beside her in the dining room and wrapped his arms around her. "Oh god, I'm such and idiot. I'm so sorry. I didn't know."

He held her as she bawled, apologizing and occasionally reaching out to wipe her hair back out of her face. "I'm so sorry, Lo. I didn't know," he said over and over again, not knowing what else to say.

Lauren cried until her head and throat throbbed and her eyes ran out of tears. Jason waited patiently through the release—a release that taught them both a very valuable lesson in their marriage: the very hardest parts of "hard times" were the parts you never even admitted to.

Once she was able to breathe normally again, Lauren used her first bit of breath as only she would—to try and gain back some sense of control. She clutched the arm Jason had placed around her shoulder, and through lips that felt numb from crying began to speak. "Me wanting to get the window fixed is a normal, legitimate concern."

"It is," Jason agreed. "You don't need me to tell you that."

"No, I don't."

Lauren wiped at her tears with the back of her hands in an attempt to pull herself together. She craned her head up to check on Landon in the living room. She couldn't help but to laugh lightly when she saw him. The baby had somehow managed to nod off during all of the commotion.

"Am I gonna screw him up?" she asked.

"You're going to be the one reason, no matter what, he never gets screwed up." Jason reached out and cupped his wife's face in his hands. "When you love someone that much, you don't let them fall."

Lauren returned her husband's gaze. She could see tears in his eyes as well.

"I haven't once thought about how you've been affected by all this," Lauren said, embarrassed. "How awful is that?"

Jason stopped her. "No, that's not on you. This isn't about me. I love you. We'll lock up extra tight and get that window

fixed. We have Halloween tomorrow. You love Halloween."
Lauren nodded.

"It's gonna be fine," Jason reassured her. "Everything's going to be just fine."

During Lauren and Jason's entire argument, Derek remained motionless under their bed. He was lost, staring into the dark eyes of his mother's now lifeless body next to him. It wasn't until about an hour later—when the Scotts had collected themselves enough to be able to leave for their jobs—that Derek finally slid out from underneath the mattress. He stood watching from behind the sheer curtains of the living room window as "his" family pulled out of the driveway. He gripped the sheet under his arm and grasped the knife in his hand tightly. Angela, now badly decomposing, walked up behind him.

"It's not going to work," she said flatly. "They know what you did now."

Chapter 13

Angela threw the car door open before the car even came to a full stop in front of Derek's school. She was strung out and sweating heavily. As she marched down the building's empty main hallway, her determined flat footsteps echoed behind her like the impatient bouncing of a child's ball. Her head twisted in a grotesque fashion as she peered into every classroom that she passed. When Angela passed Ms. Wendy's classroom, she stopped dead in her tracks—she could see them inside. Ms. Wendy sat quietly at her desk, grading papers. Derek sat in his seat finishing up a worksheet she had given him to complete.

"Who the hell do you think you are?!"

Ms. Wendy jumped back in her chair as Angela roared into the classroom. Derek shrank back in his seat as his mother pointed at him.

"You have absolutely no right to put those ideas in my son's head!"

Ms. Wendy stumbled as she stood up from her seat. "I'm

sorry, but..."

"Derek is *not* white trash and he doesn't need your damn charity."

"Of course not." Ms. Wendy tried to remain demure and collected, but the kindness in her voice only fueled Angela's rage. "I didn't mean to give that impression," Ms. Wendy continued. "Mrs. Fisher, I'm only trying to...help."

"Help? *Help*?!" Angela snorted. "Keeping him after school, feeding him lunch, all your private little conversations, and now you want to whisk him away on a trip? What kind of teacher, no—what kind of *person*, are you?! I should be calling the damn cops on you!"

"Excuse me? What exactly are you insinuating?" Ms. Wendy's voice trembled as she spoke. "You have absolutely no right to accuse me of...I would never..."

"I have every right! I'm his mother. I have done everything for that damn child. I will not have you filling his head with this garbage!"

"As his teacher..."

"As his teacher," Angela said, mimicking Ms. Wendy's voice in an insulting, high-pitched tone. "Well, guess what? You're not his teacher anymore." Angela flew toward her son and grabbed him by the back of the shirt. As she hauled him up, Angela screamed, "This school has done nothing for him! Anything he needs to know, he'll learn from me!"

Derek dutifully followed his mother to the door.

Ms. Wendy followed them. "Don't..."

Angela wheeled around to stop her. "One more step toward my son and I'll slap you with a sexual misconduct lawsuit so fast it'll make your head spin."

Ms. Wendy froze at the charges now being waved in front of her, and Angela delighted in the fear she saw in the teacher's eyes. "Doesn't matter if I win, you know that. People will always wonder. People will always talk. You wanna end your career right now or not?"

Ms. Wendy held her stance briefly, but Angela's eyes burned into her, unflinching, until she finally called the teacher's bluff. Ms. Wendy took a step back and raised her hands in a sign of surrender. She understood far too well what an accusation like that would mean. Everyone has a breaking point. She cared, she did, but putting her career and her reputation on the line was further than she was willing to go—even for her favorite student. Triumphant, Angela smiled a crooked smile, grabbed Derek by the arm and led him out of the classroom. Ms. Wendy stole one last sad look at Derek as he left. He returned it with nothing more than a meek, sideways glance.

Chapter 14

Still in a fog from the morning's unsettling discovery of the cat, Lauren stood motionless in front of the grocery store's Halloween candy display. The store was quite crowded being that it was the night before Halloween. A man bumped into Lauren's shoulder as he reached around her to grab for a particular bag of candy.

"Oh, sorry," Lauren said to the stranger as she woke from her daze. Lauren reached forward to grab a bag of candies in the shape of tiny pumpkins when another person bumped into her.

"Excuse me," the pretty, young blonde said to Lauren. Lauren was about to say how it was no problem when the woman spotted someone she knew behind her.

"Wendy?! *Hiii!*" the blonde squealed happily, knocking Lauren aside to hug her friend. "Don't you look cute! What are you doin' here?"

"Oh, just gettin' candy for my class tomorrow."

Lauren cringed at the women's twangy bubbly voices. She hastily grabbed a few bags of candy and threw them into her cart. But just as Lauren turned to go, the blonde woman said something to her friend that stopped Lauren cold.

"Hey, don't you teach where that kid who killed his mom went?! The Fisher kid?"

Lauren felt the hair rise on the back of her neck.

"He most certainly did *not* kill that woman," Wendy replied, indignant.

"Wait, you actually knew him?"

The two women looked over at Lauren who hadn't even realized she was staring at them. Lauren quickly turned around and picked up another bag of candy from a display near her. She turned the package of Halloween candy over in her hands and pretended to read the nutritional label. Wendy lowered her voice—speaking confidentially to her friend—but Lauren was close enough that she was still able to make out what they were saying.

"He was my student. Gentle as a lamb. Wouldn't hurt a soul. His mother on the other hand? Pure evil," Wendy said intensely. "For the life of me I'll never understand how nobody ever took that boy out of that home!"

"Did you ever report her?" Her friend asked.

"Me? Well…no," Wendy floundered, sounding like she couldn't get off the subject fast enough. "It's an educator thing. It's more complicated than it seems."

"No, I bet! Well, bless his heart," the blonde breathed enthusiastically. "The news sure is making it look like he did it."

"Let's just say if he did kill her, he was protectin' himself. I'd put my very own life down on that. And that's a fact. My lips to God's..." Wendy trailed off. She turned to face Lauren who once again had forgotten herself and was staring directly at the two women.

"You with the press or somethin'?" Wendy asked.

"Oh, me?" Lauren was embarrassed, but she knew there was no sense denying she was listening this time. "No, I'm not with the press."

Ms. Wendy fluffed her hair with her hand. "Too bad. They never want to talk to you when you're having a good hair day," she said, laughing to her friend.

Lauren smiled in spite of herself. This Wendy woman had a certain charm about her.

"Did you know him?" Wendy asked Lauren.

"Oh, no." Lauren shook her head. "Nothing like that."

The pretty blonde friend chimed in, "So if you aren't the press and you don't know him, why do you care then?"

Lauren shrugged. "I guess, I'm starting to wonder why more people don't."

Chapter 15

Halloween day arrived without incident. In the morning, Derek worked away in his crawl space. He cleaned. He organized. He agonized over the best way to display the items he'd so carefully collected from the Scotts' home that week. Still, everything felt off. The perfect flow of the river had been interrupted; Derek found his thoughts becoming increasingly more disjointed.

At one point during the day while Jason and Lauren were at work, he thought he heard a car pull into the back yard of the Scotts' home. When he peeked through the wire mesh of an air vent, he was surprised to see Ms. Wendy. She wasn't standing in the Scotts' yard, though. When he looked through the vent, Derek saw Ms. Wendy standing in the front yard of his trailer home. Derek tried waving to her, but Ms. Wendy didn't see him. She walked halfway toward the house, hesitated as if she had lost her nerve, then returned to her car and drove off. As Ms. Wendy drove away, Derek couldn't help but feel like everything he'd worked so hard for was going with her. In an attempt to keep his sorrows at bay, Derek went straight for the knife and sheet he'd taken from the Scotts' home. *It was time*, he thought. That night, the Scotts would have to accept him.

With the baby dressed as a pirate on his hip, Jason stared impatiently out of the windows by the front door.

"Come on, babe, we gotta go," he called out to his wife. Lauren was frantically searching for something she couldn't find in the living room.

"I swear, I *swear* I left it in here," she said partially to herself, partially to her husband.

"Left what? Come on, we wanna go trick-or-treating. I see kids out there already."

Lauren had decorated the living room with cobwebs, flashing lights, and robotic ghouls and goblins that automatically let out shrieks and screams as she weaved around them. Lauren sighed in defeat as she gave up her search.

"Well, I think we have a real life ghost in this house, Jason..."

"Can you refer to a ghost as 'real life'?"

"No, I'm serious! Not only has my favorite lipstick vanished out of my drawer, but now I can't find my black scarf. I remember putting that scarf right here in the living room before I left for work this morning. *And* now my cell phone is missing, too."

"The cell phone you're holding in your hand?" Jason asked.

"What?" Lauren looked down at the cell phone in her hand and groaned. "Oh, my god." She laughed in spite of herself. "Well, that's embarrassing."

Lauren shook her head and grabbed an eye patch and pirate hat off the sofa before joining Jason and the baby at the front door. "But that still doesn't explain the lipstick and scarf."

Jason smiled impishly at his wife. "If we're going to be haunted, I'd say a ghost that steals make-up and scarves isn't the worst we could do."

Lauren only half-jokingly smashed the adult-sized pirate hat down on Jason's head, then stretched the elastic band of the eye patch around her own head.

"Seriously, though," Lauren continued, unable to shake what was bothering her. "I've just had this weird feeling lately. Something feels off…"

"Yesterday was a lot with the cops and the cat and everything," Jason replied, calmly.

"No, I know what you're saying. It's not that. It started before yesterday. It feels like…I dunno…sorta like I'm being watched. Is that weird?"

"Maybe it's something you want to talk to the therapist about," Jason said, with no judgment in his voice.

"Maybe. You really don't feel it?"

Jason shrugged. "I think it's just normal 'baby brain'. I

told Judy at work yesterday to turn the *tree* down 'cause it felt too cold in the building."

"Really?" Lauren giggled, somewhat relieved upon hearing his story.

"Just wait eighteen years 'til we sleep a full night again, and then it'll all be better."

"You're funny." Lauren adjusted Jason's hat and smiled. "And terribly cute."

Kissing Landon on the cheek, Lauren regained her composure. "Okay, let's go. Just the neighbors, right? Landon doesn't know what's going on, anyway."

"Maybe a few more."

From the doorway, Lauren looked back at the living room. "I spent two hours putting this haunted house together. I wanna get back fast, so I can actually use it on some real trick-or-treaters."

Stabbing the knife into the carefully laid out sheet that was placed on the ground in front of him, Derek twisted the blade in crude, wide circles. What the knife couldn't accomplish, he used his hands for; he ripped and stretched the fabric. When he was finished, he sat back and smiled, surveying his work. It was perfect.

A chorus of children's voices could be heard laughing and screaming in the distance as Derek pushed the door to the crawl space open and slipped out into the cool evening air.

Sliding the sheet over his head, Derek ran along the side of the house and up the Scotts' driveway. When he reached the street, he slid seamlessly into a group of ten or so trick-or-treaters.

"Cool ghost costume, dude!" one of the kids—a boy dressed as a ninja—called out as Derek joined them.

Derek beamed from under the sheet. He ran with the kids from house to house, laughing, spinning, and buzzing. Their voices circled him, their bodies bumped into his playfully. For the first time in his life, Derek let himself get lost in a good kind of chaos. Only when he saw the Scotts pass him on the opposite side of the street did Derek slow down and separate himself from the pack. The family appeared to be heading back home. Derek looked longingly at Lauren, who had her arm around her husband's waist. Landon was crying against Jason's chest. Derek slowly crossed the street and joined another group of trick-or-treaters that were following not far behind the Scotts.

"Well, that went well," Jason joked as he carried a shriek-ing Landon in through the front door. "Landon may forever be traumatized by the seven-foot werewolf at that last place."

"It's just crazy out there! Who knew there were so many kids in the neighborhood?" Lauren shut the door behind them and ran into the kitchen. "Dim the lights, will ya? Oh, and get Landon's carrier seat! A huge wave of kids are coming!"

Lauren grabbed two bowls of candy from the kitchen

counter. As she hurried to place the candy in the decorated living room, the doorbell rang.

"Oh my gosh! I should have bought more candy!"

Lauren smoothed down her pirate outfit with her hands and exhaled deeply as she walked to the door. Opening the door, she saw nearly a dozen children dressed in different costumes standing in wait.

"Oh, wow! Look at all of you! Come on in! Pick any candy you like!" Lauren said, happily. Excited murmurs followed from the group of children as they explored the mysterious set-up before them with their eyes. As Lauren led the throng of children into the decked out "haunted" living room, Jason came out of the nursery carrying Landon, who was still upset, in his carrier seat.

"Jason, I thought I asked you to dim the lights?" Lauren shook her finger at the dimmer switch on the wall next to the front door. Overly excited, the trick-or-treaters bumped into Jason as he set Landon's carrier seat down on the coffee table in the living room close to where Lauren stood. Landon kicked his feet wildly, overwhelmed by so much stimulation. Jason was so distracted by all the commotion—the beehive of children marveling at the haunted living room and trying to assist Lauren—he failed to notice that he had forgotten to buckle Landon into the seat. All the decorations took on new life as Jason dimmed the lights. Witch statues cackled. Children shrieked, delighted with Lauren's efforts.

The doorbell rang again.

"I'll get it," Lauren said to Jason over the children's chattering and the electronic ghouls wailing. Jason moved back into the living room with the kids while Lauren swung around to greet the next round of trick-or-treaters at the door.

"Come on in!" she called out to two adorable little cheerleaders with pigtails. Lauren waved the girls in, smiling, but froze as she turned back to the doorway. Standing there alone was a fairly tall person with a sheet over their head. Lauren could make out the brown eyes of the person through the holes in the sheet, but she couldn't tell if they were a child, adult, boy or girl. Lauren didn't know why, but she felt goosebumps break out all over her body. She and the person wearing the sheet stared at one another until it felt too long. Uncomfortable, Lauren forced herself to break the silence.

"Quite the costume. Old school."

The ghost didn't say anything back.

Lauren stepped to the side and held her hand out toward the candy. "Well, come on in."

The ghost took a slow step over the threshold when suddenly he was rushed from behind by another wave of children. Not waiting for an invitation, the children ran around the ghost, excited to join the rest of the kids already in the house. Lauren and Jason tried to direct the rush of traffic as best they could, but with so many kids in the house all at once, they were losing control.

Derek awkwardly followed the swarm of children inside, but didn't run to the candy bowls and statues with them. Instead, he hung back, peering out through the holes of his sheet, observing. Derek's eyes locked on Landon. On the coffee table in front of him, the baby kicked restlessly in his seat. Jason and Lauren were too distracted by the crowd to notice how, with every thrust of his little legs, the baby's seat was inching ever closer to the edge of the table. As Derek focused in on the baby, three more kids in costume came bursting through the front door. As the children rushed past him, one of the kids accidentally bumped into the side of Landon's carrier seat. The bump was the last little shove the seat needed to send it tumbling off the edge of the table. The only one seeing what was happening, Derek immediately leapt forward. He caught the baby in his hands midair just before Landon would have crashed head first into the hardwood floor below. The crowd parted and Lauren shrieked. She saw the whole scene unfold as if it were in slow-motion.

"Oh! Oh, my god!" Lauren cried out as she ran across the room to Derek. Instead of handing the baby back to her, Derek turned away from Lauren and lifted the baby out towards Jason. Derek's sheet had become disheveled in all the action and he removed it fully, as he handed the infant back to its father. Lauren was so beside herself, the anticipatory action didn't strike her as peculiar at all.

"Everything's okay," Jason assured the stunned crowd of

trick-or-treaters. "Maybe we should move this outside, kids."

Jason paused in front of Derek who, with his sheet now off, was fully revealed to him. "Thank you, young man," he said as he ushered the children back outside.

Jason shifted Landon to the side of his body farthest away from Derek and extended his hand to him. Derek's chest puffed out as he accepted the handshake.

"Good grip there. You play football?" Jason joked. Derek shook his head back and forth with wide eyes. Jason ruffled Derek's hair and winked at him. "Thanks again. You're a good kid."

Cautiously, Lauren approached the two of them with the carrier in her arms. "Yes, thank you so much," she agreed.

After a quick inspection of the baby for any bumps or bruises, Lauren held the carrier out for Jason to put Landon inside. Derek beamed brightly at her.

Another round of trick-or-treaters arrived at the door, and as Lauren took the baby, Jason attempted to keep them at bay. "Get me the candy bowl will ya, Lauren? Sorry, kids! We're gonna keep this outside the rest of the night."

"Aw!" the crowd collectively called out, disappointed.

Lauren handed Jason the bowl of candy, flashed Derek another grateful smile, then dutifully whisked Landon back to his room. Derek noticed Lauren giving the baby a final once-over for injuries as she walked away with him. The excitement of the moment died down almost as quickly as it had come on, but Derek was still spinning inside. He remained standing awkwardly in the living room as Jason attended to the trick-or-treaters at the door. Looking back into the living room after handing out candy, Jason was surprised to still see the boy standing there.

"Oh, sorry. You probably didn't get any candy did you?" Jason held the bowl out to Derek. "Take as much as you want. You've earned it."

Derek fished his hand in the bowl and pulled out one small piece of candy.

"That's it?" Jason asked surprised. "Man, you really are a great kid, you know that?"

Derek felt his heart swell.

"Really, thanks again."

Derek smiled but stayed firmly rooted to his spot. Jason continued to thank him until there was nothing left to say.

"Trick or treat!" a fresh round of tiny voices called from behind them.

"Have a good night, kid," Jason said to Derek. There was a finality to his voice this time. "You better get going. Plenty more houses you need to visit."

Before Derek could leave or respond to this polite dismissal of his services, more excited shrieks burst forth from the entryway. As Jason turned to acknowledge the children, Derek shifted his weight nervously from one leg to the other in the living room. Although familiar to him, everything about the empty family room felt off to Derek now. It wasn't comfortable.

Why isn't the house protecting me? It led me here. I'm supposed to be here. It's my destiny. Derek's thoughts raced. *Why am I being pushed out?* Derek searched the walls for answers—for its life—but he came up empty handed. The house ignored him; they were just walls. *Oh no!* Derek panicked. *What if I'm wrong about everything?* He could feel his breath start to quicken. And desperate to find something—anything— to ground him, Derek zoned in on the beautiful black and white family portrait of the Scotts that sat on the side table by their fireplace. With Jason's back to him, Derek took advantage of the opportunity. He glanced down at the ghost costume in his hand and took a few swift steps backward toward the photograph. When he reached the picture, Derek slid the photo into the waistband of his jeans and hastily threw his sheet back over his head.

Coming back from putting Landon down in his crib, Lauren was taken aback when she saw the ghost boy still standing in their living room.

"Don't you need to get going?" Lauren meant to be polite, but her surprise, and something else she couldn't quite put her finger on, made the question come out a little more roughly than she had intended. Before she had a chance to apologize, the ghost whizzed past her and Jason, out of their front door and into the night.

Later that night, lying on his back in the crawl space, Derek stared up into the ceiling above him as he listened to the Scotts. They had their windows open, letting in the cool night breeze. Derek could tell from their voices that they were sitting at their kitchen table.

"Guess the trick was on us," Jason griped.

"I don't get it!" Lauren argued. "Why would kids steal a picture of us?"

"'Cause they don't have anything better to do, that's why. That's the last time we're letting kids into the house for Halloween."

Derek brushed his hand across the photograph the Scotts were talking about, lovingly. He'd wanted this picture from the first time he saw it. Lauren's face in the photo reminded him of the first time he saw *her* five months earlier; it was the whole reason he'd been drawn to the home in the first place.

Chapter 16

It was garbage day and dozens of bright, unnaturally green garbage receptacles neatly lined the curbs in the cozy suburban neighborhood.

"Look at this!" Angela cried as she crawled back into the driver's side seat next to Derek. "A perfectly good lamp!"

Derek didn't acknowledge her. He stared dead-eyed out of the car's passenger side window. It had nearly been a year and a half since Angela had pulled him out of school. She had decided shortly after marching up to his school to confront Ms. Wendy that street smarts would serve him far better than book smarts in the "real world." Angela successfully silenced any curious truancy officer with, "I'm homeschooling him."

He'd begun his new education under Angela's watchful eye selling cartons of cigarettes and small amounts of marijuana to teens around the nearby trailer park. He did well, and soon "graduated" to running harder drugs with his mother's help. Angela's nasty habit of dipping into their product prompted her supplier to cut her off—but not before teaching her a lesson that had her looking as if she'd gone head to head with a professional fighter. The incident laid Angela up for the better part of a month. When she recovered, Angela made the prudent decision to switch to "less volatile" money making opportunities—her favorite of which entailed crawling through trash cans in upper class neighborhoods to find things to sell out of the trunk of her car or trade at pawn shops. Derek went along for the ride sometimes but rarely participated. As he grew older, it wasn't interesting to him; not much was interesting to him anymore. Angela had no modesty about her dumpster diving. She didn't pick through the garbage in the early mornings before people were up. Instead, she boldly rode around in their beat-up old car in the middle of the day with little care for who was looking.

"See how wasteful these kinds of people are?" Angela moaned turning the ugly, white lamp over in her hands as if it were made of gold. "We could get ten bucks for this—at least!"

As Angela droned on about her precious new find, Derek let her voice fade into the background. He let his eyes and mind wander until they settled upon some movement happening in the driveway of a big brick home across the street from where they were parked. Derek watched as a fancy black car pulled into the driveway. As soon as the car stopped, Derek saw a man hop out of the driver's seat and rush around the vehicle to help a woman out of the passenger side. Derek's eyes flitted away from the couple momentarily, noticing a painted sign sitting in an easel next to the home's front door that read, "The Scotts." *The Scotts*, Derek mouthed silently to himself. Derek also took note of a big wooden stork in the home's front yard that read, "Congratulations," and a dozen or so blue latex balloons that were attached to the home's mailbox. *They must have just had a baby*, Derek surmised, unmoved by the idea.

Derek looked back toward the driveway. The man who had helped the woman out of the car was smiling and moving with a nervous and excited energy, but the woman was expressionless. Derek's eyes locked on her as the man extracted their newborn baby from the backseat with surgical-like precision. The man beamed at the woman who tried her best to smile back, but the light in her eyes was out. Derek couldn't take his eyes off of this woman. She was like him, only Derek couldn't understand—if this woman felt the same way he did, why would she try to smile?

Angela's voice came back into focus as the man and woman walked into their home with the baby for the very first time as a family. Angela peered over to examine what had taken her son's interest.

"Bet you think if you lived there, your life would be magical," Angela sneered. "Well, perfect don't live nowhere, son."

Chapter 17

In the five months that followed Derek's initial discovery of the Scotts' home, his life continued its downhill trajectory. Not that Derek or Angela were aware of how long it had been; time passed for them how time passed when you don't have milestones, photographs, or events to mark it—it passed by unnoticed. Their once tidy home was in a complete state of disrepair. Derek kicked aside the trash and empty bottles that littered the floor as he made his way to the refrigerator for something to eat. He knew the refrigerator was empty, but he opened and closed it anyway. Derek glared resentfully at his mother who was passed out on the couch in the other room. She had taken up a near permanent residence there, waking only when she needed to get high or find someone she needed to get high. Belly empty, Derek skulked back to his room and waited for the drugs in her system to wear off. *Maybe she doesn't need to eat, but I do! If that means she has to miss her next dose, so be it.* He resolved as he lay down on his mattress *She is going to feed me!* He put his hands behind his head and waited. He drifted between daydreams, his anger getting the best of him as he fantasized about how he was going to "give it to her good."

He had been lying on his mattress, staring at the ceiling for about an hour, when Derek heard Angela's cough break the silence in the trailer from the doorway. The deterioration of Angela's appearance mirrored that of their home. She had sores on her arms and face; her clothes hung loosely off her body.

"Come with me," she ordered. Derek turned to look at her and noticed his mother seemed to be missing another tooth. "Now," she hissed at his hesitation.

Derek breathed out hard as he watched Angela slip into the hallway. He was hungry and his patience was thin. Rolling off his bed, Derek followed his mother into the kitchen. She stopped when she reached the counter.

"Pick it up," Angela said as she pointed to an old home phone that hadn't been used in ages. Her voice was quiet and controlled. Derek stared back at her with her same coldness. He didn't feel like playing these games today.

"I said, pick it up."

Not moving his eyes from his mother's, Derek picked up the phone receiver and lifted it to his ear, knowing that it had long been disconnected. Angela itched at her arms, annoyed.

"Do you hear it?" she asked.

Derek listened to the silence for a moment and then held the receiver out to her. "It's dead, Mom."

"It is, is it?" Snatching the phone from her son's hand, Angela put it roughly to her ear. "Is that what they told you to say?"

Derek watched her, detached, as she slammed the phone back down on the counter.

"It's dead, is it?"

"You haven't paid the bill, Mom."

"Is that what they told you to say?!" Angela picked up the receiver again and hit him on the shoulder with it. "Is that what they told you to say?!"

Derek dodged the next couple of blows that followed, but Angela was out to do damage. She swung the phone at him over and over again like a hammer. Derek suddenly felt himself grab his mother by the shoulders. It only took one good shove and Angela was sent flying across the room. As she landed on the living room floor, Angela looked up at Derek, stunned.

At first, he was afraid; Derek had never fought back before. But as he stared at his mother on the ground, waiting for her response, Derek registered something in her eyes that shocked him—*she* was afraid. *She* was afraid of *him*. Derek may have only been fifteen, but he was taller than her now, and her wasted frame was no match for his youthful strength. Derek felt a surprising surge of power at the realization. She wasn't going to get him this time. As if she could read his thoughts, Angela snarled as she climbed to her feet. Her hair was wild and her eyes a fiery inferno that screamed of the hell there would be to pay.

"Come on in!" Lauren called out cheerfully to the balding, middle-aged repairman at the front door. "I've been dying to get this all fixed up."

"How'd it break?" The repairman asked as Lauren led him through the house to the open dining room window.

"Apparently, I don't know my own strength!" Lauren joked.

She pulled her cell phone out of her back pocket and began typing away, not at all noticing the queer look the repairman was giving her.

"I'll say," the repairman commented, scratching his head as he surveyed the snapped window latches. "Did you ever find the missing pieces?"

"Huh? Oh, can't say we did," Lauren answered, distracted. "Just hoping our little one doesn't find them first."

The repairman began making adjustments on the window, then lifted the windowpane up and out of its frame. "How old's your little one?" he asked as he placed the windowpane on the floor next to him with experienced ease.

"He's almost six months."

"A boy? Such a great age. I have a granddaughter not much older than that. Where is the little guy?"

Lauren looked up from her phone and tucked it in her back pocket. "His dad took him to pre-school already. I've got to get to work as soon as we're done here."

The repairman smiled. "Well, this won't take no time at all. I'm just gonna slide in a whole new unit and you'll be free to go."

While Lauren and the repairman engaged in their pleasantries above him, Derek paced the crawl space below. With each step, he felt as though he was trying to physically catch up with his thoughts, but no matter how fast he paced, his memories remained frustratingly out of reach. He recalled the last time he had been with his mother. Why couldn't he remember what happened next? What happened after he had pushed her? His memories were blurry. Derek paused and bit at the thumbnail of his right hand. *What happened?*

As he strained to remember, Angela's arms suddenly burst forth from the ground of the crawlspace in front of him. He stumbled backward in pure horror at the sight of her. As she scraped and ripped her way out of the damp earth, Derek could see she was covered in blood. Her throat was slashed, and bugs crawled out of the dozens of deep wounds that covered her body. She smiled at him, revealing her rotting teeth.

"What happened?" Angela asked, but the voice that came out of his mother didn't belong to her. It was a deep male's voice. It was the voice of Mike, the police officer that Derek recognized from listening while he had been concealed under the bed in the Scotts' home.

"What happened?" the voice inside of Angela asked again. "It takes a special kind of monster to do what he did to her."

Derek fell to his knees. All of the memories came crashing back to him in one blinding flash of light. He saw Angela on the floor in their trailer. He saw her getting up after he had pushed her to the ground, angry—wild. Derek saw himself grabbing a knife on the counter next to him. He was wheeling around to point it at her, to yell at her to stop, but the words were too slow. As he turned around, his mother was already charging at him. She ran hard into the blade. He hadn't meant to do it. He had only meant to use the knife to give her a serious warning: back off. She ran right into it. They were eye to eye just long enough to register each other's mutual shock. Derek immediately let go of the knife, but it stayed lodged in her body as she fell to the ground with a thud in front of him. The life exited Angela's body almost instantly. It was odd she would go like that; that she would leave the earth without any trace of the fight that had so defined her in her life. Derek fell to his knees over his mother's lifeless body. He shook her by the shoulders, but there was nothing—no movement.

"Mom?" he uttered softly.

The only response he got was the loud silence of their empty trailer. It almost seemed to echo—if silence can do such a thing. Derek put his hand over his mouth to muffle a sob. *How could she do this?* He breathed deeply and shook her again, this time harder. The movement didn't wake her. He knew she was dead, yet strangely, shaking her felt good. Derek slapped her across the face; a good solid whack. That felt even better. Derek suddenly felt all the rage he'd pushed deep down inside of himself for fifteen years rocket out of him with alarming force. All the memories of cruelty and betrayal he had pushed down somewhere deep in his mind barreled their way to the forefront.

Derek let out a guttural howl as he ripped the blade from his mother's chest and plunged it back into her over and over and over again. He shook. He couldn't stop—he *didn't* stop. He didn't stop until his muscles were too physically weak to drive the blade in anymore. It was the only way Derek felt he could fight back—to get out the frustration over what she had done. As if her years of abuse hadn't been enough, with this final act, Angela had now ruined him in every single way a person could be ruined. Her death was his death.

Lauren was pleased to finally have the window fixed.

"Thank you so much!" Lauren called out cheerfully as she closed and locked the front door behind the repairman who tipped an imaginary hat to her as he left. Pulling her cell phone from her back pocket, Lauren dialed Jason.

"Hey, babe. How was Landon when you dropped him off?" She opened the fridge and grabbed the last apple out, taking a bite as he answered, "Awwww, okay. I might stop by the school on my way to work. That was so much faster than I thought it'd be," Lauren absentmindedly chewed. "Yup, all fixed," she answered with her mouth full. "I just need to know where the deadbolt is for the crawl space. Remember you said we could lock it up for the season?" Lauren placed the apple down on the counter and walked into the garage as she continued to talk. "Two birds, one stone and all, ya know?"

Something about getting everything in the house in order made her feel like her life was getting more in order, too. Lauren felt a spring in her step as she opened the door from the kitchen to the garage.

"I know it's in the garage somewhere. Yup, I'm in here," she answered her husband as she fumbled with the light switch. "Second drawer? Hang on."

Lauren walked over to a wall in the garage where a plastic shelving unit they used as storage sat. She then pulled the second drawer open, as Jason had instructed. Sitting right where he said it would be—in the center of the drawer—was a large deadbolt and its accompanying small key.

"There it is!" Lauren chirped. Just the sight of the lock had her gleefully ticking the duty off of the imaginary checklist in her head. "Thanks, babe."

As she brought the lock inside the house, Lauren said goodbye to her husband on the phone. "I'll just throw this lock on and then I'll be headin' out." She smiled. "love you, too."

Chapter 18

Derek cowered in the far back reaches of the crawl space, trying to hide from the shadows, voices and memories that swirled around him like hungry sharks. He could feel the very foundation of the Scotts' home trembling with him. In his hands, Derek held the white latches to the Scotts' dining room window.

"Please," he prayed to the latches. "Please, help me." But the house rumbled more.

Meanwhile, completely unaware of Derek's presence below her in the dark, Lauren opened the back door to the house. The deadbolt swung lightly by her side as she made her way down the stairs toward the crawl space. When Lauren got to the door of the crawl space, however, she paused. The door was slightly ajar and she could see that the light bulb inside the crawl space was turned on. *Well that's weird,* she thought. Lauren pushed the door open a little bit more, but as she reached her hand forward to turn off the light, she froze.

What the…? Lauren blinked hard a few times just to be sure that what she was seeing was real. All of the junk stored under their home had been moved around, and the placement of everything was…strangely familiar. She studied what she was seeing for a moment. *It's a…it's a perfect replica of our home above.* Lauren smiled, feeling puzzled. She was confused yet found the situation oddly enchanting. Was this Jason playing some kind of elaborate joke on her, she wondered? A Halloween trick perhaps? Lauren took a few tentative steps inside of the crawl space to get a better look. She shook her head in amused disbelief. In front of her were flowers in a plastic cup on what was supposed to be the "dining" table. They were the same flowers she currently had sitting in a vase on the dining table in the house. *What is Jason up to?* she thought.

When Lauren looked to her left, she recognized the extra blankets she usually kept stored in the linen closet were now draped over storage bins that had been set up to look like their living room furniture. Lauren chuckled to herself. *This is crazy!* The black, plastic moisture barrier on the ground shifted beneath her feet as she moved further into the model of her living room. She noticed that even the moisture barrier looked like it had been cleaned! As she turned to look around, Lauren began to take notice of some of the items she thought had gone missing from the house. They were scattered all around her. *What? Had Jason been taking them down here all along? But why would he…*

Lauren stiffened.

Something sitting on an old shelf, near where the fireplace would be in the make-believe room, sent shivers down her spine. It was the black and white family photo that had been taken from their home on Halloween, the night before. She had been with Jason all night. He had never left the house. *How could he have...* Before Lauren could finish her thought, Derek stumbled out from the shadows where he had been watching her.

Lauren felt the color drain from her face as the form that emerged from the darkness began to take shape. Her heart seized in her chest as she looked at the boy in front of her. Her mind suddenly raced as it worked overtime to make the connection. She knew him. It was the boy—the boy dressed as the ghost! The one who had helped Landon. *What is he doing down here?!* Derek approached her slowly with a sad smile. He had his arms outstretched at his sides, palms toward her, to imply he didn't mean any harm.

"I didn't mean to," Derek said with resignation. "I didn't mean to kill my mom."

Time seemed to slow and stretch as the words came out of his mouth. They were only two small sentences, but the words were so significant they pieced a complete story together with lightning speed. In an instant, Lauren shot out of the crawl space, slamming the door shut behind her. Her hands shook as she slid the deadbolt into place and locked it.

As Lauren stumbled up the steps to the house, she heard Derek scream through the door. "Wait! Please. I'm not going to hurt you. Please!"

Lauren crashed into the house, then frantically locked the back door behind her. Her heart raced as she yanked her cell phone from her pocket.

"Nine one one. What is your emergency?" she heard the young, female operator ask.

"Yes, I have an intruder at my home. Seven four nine Grandview Drive. He's below my house. I think he's someone...he's someone the police are looking for. He killed his mom. Please...please send someone."

"You said the intruder is outside?" The operator's voice was direct and controlled.

Lauren flew around the home, making sure all of the doors and windows were locked. Below her, Derek rattled the door to the locked crawl space desperately.

"Is this man armed?" the operator asked Lauren through the phone.

The word "man" struck Lauren. She flashed back to the doe-eyed young boy who had stood so proudly in front of her in her living room only the night before.

"Man? No, he's not a man...I mean, no, he's not armed."

"Okay, ma'am. We have help on the way. I'm going to stay on the phone with you until they get there. Are your doors locked?"

"Yes, they're…" Lauren trailed off. What she was seeing made no sense. *Are the walls moving?* She thought to herself incredulously. If ever there was a moment she felt crazy in the past it was certainly dwarfed by what she was feeling right now. She could swear not only were the walls around her pulsating, they seemed to glow.

"Ma'am, are you still there?"

"Yeah, I uh…" Lauren cocked her head to the side, examining her surroundings. Items around the home began to shimmer with an odd silvery light; the toys strewn on the floor, the hot coffee in the pot that she and Jason couldn't start their day without, and the candle in the kitchen that smelled exactly like the cookies her grandmother used to bake. *What is happening?* She felt like she was spinning.

"Ma'am?" The operator asked again. Lauren rubbed at her eyes with her free hand. The light in the home went away.

"Yeah, I'm here," Lauren stammered. "The doors are locked. You don't need to stay on the phone. I'm fine. Just send someone, please."

Lauren hung up on the operator. She had to bend forward to catch her breath. She didn't like this. She didn't like this at all. Why did she suddenly feel so wrong about calling the police? Like she was tattling on someone? It was how he had said, "I didn't mean to kill my mom." It was such a horrible sentence, but the way he had said it—Lauren could feel that he was telling the truth. *This is ridiculous!* She argued with herself. *Someone broke into my house. There's nothing to feel bad about. Why do I feel bad?!*

She was starting to hyperventilate. Lauren knew she needed to keep her wits about her. She felt a strong rush to her head as she pushed her hands against her thighs to straighten back up. Standing made her feel a bit more grounded, but she still couldn't shake loose the absurd pangs of guilt she was feeling. Pressing her phone to her chin, she began to pace the house. She needed to assess this bizarre situation. She needed to make sense of what she was feeling. *This is a kid, not a man—a kid who's probably seen things in his life that I can't even possibly begin to imagine,* she deliberated. For a second she reasoned that that his youth excused nothing he had chosen to do, but it wasn't what seemed to bother her the most. *What would happen to him? Would the doe-eyed boy be sent to prison with grown men? What would happen to him there? That's the thing—he doesn't look like some hardened criminal. He looks like he could be...well, he looks like he could be my kid.*

Lauren moved past the sofa, scanning the living room feeling anxious. She then walked into Landon's room. There was a soft, white blanket hung neatly on the end of Landon's crib. Lauren picked it up but then put it back down. She was searching for something, but she didn't know what. The words of the woman she had seen in the grocery store—the one who said she had been the boy's teacher—played on a loop in her head. "Let's just say if he did kill her, he was protectin' himself. I'd put my very own life down on that."

Lauren made her way back into the kitchen and paused to listen. She could faintly make out the screaming coming from the floorboards beneath her. Derek was crying and screaming out to her to help him.

"I'll be good! I promise! Please! I didn't mean to! Please don't do this!"

Maybe it was instinctual—a mother responding to the cries of a child—but Lauren suddenly felt a surprising and overwhelming need to help the boy. It wasn't safe. It wasn't rational. But dammit, if it wasn't what every single cell inside her body was screaming at her to be right! Lauren stumbled around and opened the refrigerator behind her. It was the first thing she could think to do. She grabbed the mayonnaise, cheese, and deli meat and threw it all onto the counter. Then she reached for the bread, where she kept it on top of the fridge and plucked a knife out of the silverware drawer. Lauren's hands shook as she assembled the sandwich.

Derek screamed so loudly, the floor beneath Lauren seemed to vibrate. "*Please,*" he begged, his cries filled with anguish.

Lauren felt her throat tighten. She smashed the top piece of bread down on the sloppy turkey sandwich in front of her, and hung her head. *It's not enough,* she told herself. *It's not enough. It's not enough.* Lauren's heart pounded and ached at the same time; it was excruciating. She looked over her shoulder at a picture of her son and husband stuck to the refrigerator with an alphabet magnet. She smiled, pained by the picture, then made her way to the pantry where she pulled out a brown paper bag. Placing the sandwich gently in the bag, Lauren walked stoically to the back door. She pressed her ear to the glass. The boy wasn't screaming anymore. Taking a deep breath, Lauren unlocked the door and stepped outside into the crisp morning air. Derek could hear the footsteps coming down the stairs and whimpered when they came to a stop right outside of the crawl space door.

"Hello?" Lauren called out. Her voice was soft and unsure. She wanted to say something to him but didn't know what. She cautiously reached out to touch the crawl space door in front of her. Under her fingers, the door's peeling white paint felt rough. "The police are coming," she said to Derek through the crawl space door.

Lauren tried to speak again, but her voice cracked and nothing would come out. Derek reached out his hand and placed it on the other side of the door.

"Why did you do that?" His voice was soft, like a lamb's.

Lauren's head fell forward.

"I'm sorry," she said as she choked back a sob. Lauren eyed the deadbolt in front of her. "Sometimes we need more than what other people can give us."

"Please," Derek begged. "Please. I won't do anything bad.

I didn't mean to. I promise I won't hurt you. Please don't lock me in here."

Lauren felt the tears stream hot on her face. They rolled freely down her cheeks and onto her shirt. She cautiously moved her hand down to the door's deadbolt. The chilly fall air had made the metal cold. As she twisted the lock around in her fingers, she noticed it still had the key in it. When she'd locked it before, she had forgotten to take it with her because of all the excitement.

"I have a family," she begged back. "I can't."

"I promise I'll go. Just let me go."

Just then, police sirens roared into the neighborhood. Derek's whimpers grew from behind the door. Lauren whipped her head back to look at the woods behind her house then turned her gaze back to the lock in front of her. She felt her hands begin to twist the key in the deadbolt. *Why am I doing this? I shouldn't be doing this!* She screamed inwardly, but she didn't stop. The deadbolt clicked as the lock came undone. She slipped the deadbolt out of the door and tossed it on the ground with a thud.

Lauren looked at the door in front of her, waiting for something to happen. She heard something—Derek moving behind the door. Her eyes went wide as she realized what she was hearing. It was the undeniable sound of someone charging directly towards her. The now unlocked door slammed hard into Lauren as Derek threw his entire weight against it. She flew to the ground. The brown paper sack she had been holding landed in the grass next to her.

Terrified, Lauren used her arms to crawl backwards away from Derek who now towered over her. Even in her panicked state, somewhere in Lauren's mind, she was still able to register the sounds of police sirens and car doors slamming in front of the house. As the two stared at each other, Lauren realized Derek was just as scared as she was. Derek looked down at the lunch bag on the ground next to her. The turkey sandwich Lauren had made for him had fallen halfway out of the bag and onto the grass.

"Was that for me?"

Lauren didn't answer him. Instead, she nodded over her shoulder at the tree line behind them. "Run," she whispered.

Derek reached his hand out to her. "Here, let me help you."

Tears stung Lauren's eyes immediately. She felt the meaning of the universe in that one simple gesture of kindness. How did it ever come to be that this poor, tortured young soul was extending a hand, so that he could help *her* up? Lauren felt the heartbeat of something other-worldly as she placed her hand in Derek's and looked up into his face, but as he pulled her toward him…

Pop, pop, pop.

Derek's eyes went wide and Lauren let out a piercing scream as she watched Derek's shirt fill with blood. His body fell forward onto her, revealing three officers with guns drawn behind him.

"Get out of there!" A voice boomed from behind. Lauren saw one of the officers, a man she immediately recognized as Mike, frantically waving his arm at her to move out of the way. "Ma'am, get out of there!"

Lauren's body began to quake. She *did* start to move, but not away. She moved toward Derek. Sobbing, she latched onto the boy. She rocked him. Lauren rocked the boy the way all children deserved to be. She felt the officers pulling and tugging at her arms, but Lauren held fast. She wasn't about to let the boy leave the earth without knowing what it felt like to be truly held. Time, sound, light, and noise slipped away. Everything slipped away, except for the one thing that mattered—love.

Chapter 19

Many hours and interviews later, Lauren stood feeling completely and utterly drained. She stared out of the living room window of her beautiful brick house on Grandview Drive. Jason put his arm around her as the last of the police cars drove away.

"You okay?"

Lauren said nothing. She held the black and white family photo Derek had stolen of them to her chest.

"You did everything right," Jason tried to reassure her. "He broke into our home, Lauren."

Lauren held up her hand. "Just stop," she said quietly.

"It's not your fault. You couldn't save him."

"Who could have? After what the police told us about him?" Lauren shook her head, her eyes welling up with tears. "Is this what happens to people who don't have somebody? Because of some messed up, cosmic lottery nobody understands...that decides where and who we're born to? And we all just sit back and say, 'Oh well, that's what happens to people like that'." Lauren lifted her eyes to Jason. "How is that right? Tell me how that's right."

Jason shook his head. "It's not," he replied.

Still clutching their family photo to her body, Lauren used her free hand to reach out and gently touch the side of her husband's face. "I'm so lucky I have you," she said. "I know that. I want you to know, I know that."

Jason grabbed her hand and gave it a squeeze and a kiss. "I love you, too."

As Lauren pulled her hand back, she smiled sweetly at him and said, "Why don't you go lie down? I'll be there in a minute." It had been one of the longest days of her life, for Jason, too.

"Sure," Jason agreed. "Lemme just go check on Landon one last time."

As he moved to walk past her to the baby's room, Lauren stopped him. "No, I'll do it."

Jason looked at her with surprise. "You sure?"

"Yeah," Lauren nodded. "I am. I can't make any promises that everything's going to be great from here on out or anything, but I want to. "

"If you need help, it's no big deal."

"I know." She held up the family photo in her hand. "Just need to put this back first."

Jason smiled. "Okay."

As Jason walked back to their bedroom to give Lauren her space, she ran her hand slowly over the image of her family. She'd never realized how sad she'd looked in the photo before. *We'll have to take another one*, she thought as she moved to put it back where Derek had taken it from on the side table near the fireplace. As she crossed in front of the fireplace, however, something else caught her eye. Lauren stared deeply into the ornate, Fabergé-esque egg—her most prized possession—proudly displayed on the mantle in front of her. Reaching her hand out, Lauren touched it with her fingers and tipped the egg over. The shell instantly shattered into hundreds of pieces as it crashed to the floor. She lifted the photograph in her hand and delicately placed her family where the egg had always been—in the center of her home.

About the Author

Natalie Roers is an award-winning author, voice over artist, and veteran radio and television personality. She is the author of the young adult fantasy, *Lucid,* and popular broadcast-industry guide, *How to Become a Voice-Over Artist.* To learn more about her, please visit www.natalieroers.com.

If you enjoyed this book, please post a review at your favorite online bookstore.

If you enjoyed *Beneath Them,* consider these other fine books from
Aignos Publishing:

The Dark Side of Sunshine by Paul Guzzo
Happy that it's Not True by Carlos Aleman
Cazadores de Libros Perdidos by German Barber [Spanish]
The Desert and the City by Derek Bickerton
The Overnight Family Man by Paul Guzzo
There is No Cholera in Zimbabwe by Zachary M. Oliver
John Doe by Buz Sawyers
The Piano Tuner's Wife by Jean Yamasaki Toyama
Nuno by Carlos Aleman
*An Aura of Greatness: Reflections on Governor John A. Burn*s
by Brendan P. Burns
Polonio Pass by Doc Krinberg
Iwana by Alvaro Leiva
University and King by Jeffrey Ryan Long
The Surreal Adventures of Dr. Mingus by Jesus Richard Felix Rodriguez
Letters by Buz Sawyers
In the Heart of the Country by Derek Bickerton
El Camino De Regreso by Maricruz Acuna [Spanish]
Diego in Two Places by Carlos Aleman
Prepositions by Jean Yamasaki Toyama
Deep Slumber of Dogs by Doc Krinberg
Saddam's Parrot by Jim Currie

Coming Soon:
Chang The Magic Cat by A. G. Hayes

Aignos Publishing | an imprint of Savant Books and Publications
www.aignospublishing.com

as well as these other fine books from Savant Books and Publications:

Essay, Essay, Essay by Yasuo Kobachi
Aloha from Coffee Island by Walter Miyanari
Footprints, Smiles and Little White Lies by Daniel S. Janik
The Illustrated Middle Earth by Daniel S. Janik
Last and Final Harvest by Daniel S. Janik
A Whale's Tale by Daniel S. Janik
Tropic of California by R. Page Kaufman
Tropic of California (the companion music CD) by R. Page Kaufman
The Village Curtain by Tony Tame
Dare to Love in Oz by William Maltese
The Interzone by Tatsuyuki Kobayashi
Today I Am a Man by Larry Rodness
The Bahrain Conspiracy by Bentley Gates
Called Home by Gloria Schumann
Kanaka Blues by Mike Farris
First Breath edited by Z. M. Oliver
Poor Rich by Jean Blasiar
The Jumper Chronicles by W. C. Peever
William Maltese's Flicker by William Maltese
My Unborn Child by Orest Stocco
Last Song of the Whales by Four Arrows
Perilous Panacea by Ronald Klueh
Falling but Fulfilled by Zachary M. Oliver
Mythical Voyage by Robin Ymer
Hello, Norma Jean by Sue Dolleris
Richer by Jean Blasiar
Manifest Intent by Mike Farris
Charlie No Face by David B. Seaburn
Number One Bestseller by Brian Morley
My Two Wives and Three Husbands by S. Stanley Gordon
In Dire Straits by Jim Currie
Wretched Land by Mila Komarnisky
Chan Kim by Ilan Herman
Who's Killing All the Lawyers? by A. G. Hayes
Ammon's Horn by G. Amati
Wavelengths edited by Zachary M. Oliver
Almost Paradise by Laurie Hanan
Communion by Jean Blasiar and Jonathan Marcantoni
The Oil Man by Leon Puissegur
Random Views of Asia from the Mid-Pacific by William E. Sharp

The Isla Vista Crucible by Reilly Ridgell
Blood Money by Scott Mastro
In the Himalayan Nights by Anoop Chandola
On My Behalf by Helen Doan
Traveler's Rest by Jonathan Marcantoni
Keys in the River by Tendai Mwanaka
Chimney Bluffs by David B. Seaburn
The Loons by Sue Dolleris
Light Surfer by David Allan Williams
The Judas List by A. G. Hayes
Path of the Templar—Book 2 of The Jumper Chronicles by W. C. Peever
The Desperate Cycle by Tony Tame
Shutterbug by Buz Sawyer
Blessed are the Peacekeepers by Tom Donnelly and Mike Munger
B*ellwether Messages* edited by D. S. Janik
The Turtle Dances by Daniel S. Janik
The Lazarus Conspiracies by Richard Rose
Purple Haze by George B. Hudson
Imminent Danger by A. G. Hayes
Lullaby Moon (CD) by Malia Elliott of Leon & Malia
Volutions edited by Suzanne Langford
In the Eyes of the Son by Hans Brinckmann
The Hanging of Dr. Hanson by Bentley Gates
Flight of Destiny by Francis Powell
Elaine of Corbenic by Tima Z. Newman
Ballerina Birdies by Marina Yamamoto
More More Time by David B. Seabird
Crazy Like Me by Erin Lee
Cleopatra Unconquered by Helen R. Davis
Valedictory by Daniel Scott
The Chemical Factor by A. G. Hayes
Quantum Death by A. G. Hayes
Running from the Pack edited by Helen R. Davis
Big Heaven by Charlotte Hebert
Captain Riddle's Treasure by GV Rama Rao
All Things Await by Seth Clabough
Tsunami Libido by Cate Burns
Finding Kate by A. G. Hayes
The Adventures of Purple Head, Buddha Monkey and... by Erik Bracht
In the Shadows of My Mind by Andrew Massie
The Gumshoe by Richard Rose
Cereus by Z. Roux

Shadow and Light edited by Helen R. Davis

Coming Soon:

The Solar Triangle by A. G. Hayes
A Real Daughter by Lynne McKelvey
StoryTeller by Nicholas Bylotus
Bo Henry at Three Forks by Daniel D. Bradford

Savant Books and Publications
http://www.savantbooksandpublications.com

Made in the USA
Middletown, DE
13 July 2017